SOAKED HAY & FARRIER SMOKE

WHERE CLICHÉD ROMANCES ARE THE LEAST
OF YOUR WORRIES...

F.W RIDER

DEDICATION

For the man who made me start typing in the first place, My Husband, who funnily enough, actually deals with all the farrier visits for our 5 strong herd so I can write about it!

WRITTEN BY...

F. W. Rider

If you'd like to find out more about forthcoming releases or the life of my five stunning equines in general, check out my links below! You can also sign up to my free mailing list via my website!

Get to know me more here...
Instagram - https://www.
instagram.com/thefairweatherrider/
Facebook - https://www.facebook.com/thefairweatherrider
Website - http://thefairweatherrider.com

Due to the rather excessive use of profanity, graphic sexual references and adult subject matter, this book should only be read by those who aren't easily offended and should without a doubt be kept out of reach of anyone under the age of 18.

THE SOAKED HAY SMOKE & MIRRORS SERIES: BOOK 1 OF 2

Written By

F.W. Rider

Contact info@thefairweatherrider.com for more information on future releases.

ONE

THE WEATHER HAS WELL and truly turned. To say it's shitty is an understatement. In spite of what felt like a pretty mild Christmas, January has arrived and wow, has it let us know it's here. But whatever the weather, I still venture out daily and today has been no exception. I've been up since about 5 a.m. and am officially knackered. A rather looming deadline, one I've left until the very last minute – well done, me – meant waking at the crack of dawn like some nocturnal creature and hitting the keys on my Mac for a few hours.

To be fair, while I seriously loathe that immediate feeling of sheer exhaustion when your alarm goes off, getting up early and smashing out a whole chunk of work before the sun even rises is my favourite way to start the day. Not because I'm dedicated... well I guess I am a little, but mainly because it means I can drop the laptop back on the bed and head to my favourite place in the middle of the day – the yard.

Is it bad that I've always loved my own company? I don't think so, though I could do without the pitying stares that constantly come my way. I love my friends, I do. I love my family, or what family I have – just me and mum – but I also love my own company. Well, my company when I'm with my man. That man just so happens to weigh about three quarters of a tonne, have four mighty striking legs and the cutest little whiskers. That man is my warmblood Lincoln.

Today my diary is marked for the farrier visit. Yet another one of Lincoln's regular spa days as I call them. Every seven weeks on the dot, this guy gets four new shoes and I get a slightly lighter wallet. Thankfully, the sting's taken out of handing over almost £100 every seven weeks by the sheer fact that I'm secretly in love with the man who takes it. Before you say it... how cliché. Yes, yes, who'd have thought it? A horsey girl in love with the farrier, but Jesus man, the guy's a god.

I've known Eddie for years, even before Lincoln came along. I knew him as the guy who used to shoe my old loan pony before I could actually afford my own horse. It's funny because I actually began using a different farrier when I got Lincoln, who as it turns out preferred 'shoeing' of a different kind. He gave some random guy a good seeing to after a night on the sauce and got sent down for GBH.

I needed a farrier to step in at the last minute before a show and who should volunteer in all his man-mountain glory but Eddie? I'd always admired him from afar. He's a rugged kind of handsome, with a dark curly mop on top of his head and stubble to match. He also happens to be thirty - three, a little older than me, but that doesn't stop the continual spark between us. I've never had any intention of taking it further though – just the thought of being another notch on a farrier's rasp turns my stomach.

Despite telling myself that I absolutely do not want

anything to do with him aside from what he does to my boy's hooves, my appearance on farrier day is always a little less shabby.

I'd like to think it's so subtle that it's barely noticeable but it almost certainly is. Instead of turning up with my hair in a messy bun and last night's mascara on, I'm always impeccably turned out in skintight riding leggings and a tight arse base layer to highlight the figure that he absolutely will not ever lay a finger on.

The word *juvenile* obviously springs to mind, and I guess to an extent *pointless* too, considering I've already blockaded any possibility of something happening, but you know, it's nice to feel wanted and I won't lie: I do enjoy seeing his deep blue eyes wander every so often. With my very own vow of 'thou shalt not shag the farrier' firmly in my head, I still love his visits. In fact, I'd go as far as to say I long for them.

Christ, I need to get out more.

Eddie is tall enough that even in my heels – which take me to a whopping six feet – he would still tower over me. He's as wide as he is tall too. And the muscles – my God the muscles. Picking up hooves and hammering metal shoes all day long have developed his shoulders, his lats, everything. I can appreciate their aesthetics for sure, especially in the summer months, and while today unfortunately isn't a shirt-off kind of day, I can almost guarantee he'll still be down to a very tight T-shirt. Tight enough that his biceps will be doing their best to burst the seams.

Slipping on his freshly balmed leather headcollar, I lead Lincoln out of his stable and tie him up outside the barn. Eddie's reversing into his usual spot.

Lincoln as usual dives into the fresh haynet like a starved rescue case, and before I can finish the quick release knot to tie him up, he almost rips it out of my hand. I would normally be fine, but the fact that my attention has been elsewhere – i.e. on Eddie – almost lands me on my arse.

Every inch that truck moves toward me, my heart beats faster. It's embarrassing but it is what it is. I quite enjoy the vulnerability really, considering I'm usually considered quite a tough cookie to crack. I'm often asked why I'm so harsh or why I'm so tough on the outside. I don't know. I'm just independent and there's certainly nothing wrong with that.

Before he steps out of his rust bucket, I can smell him. He gives off a potent yet perfect mix of farrier smoke and sheer masculine sweat. Pair it with the sweet soaked hay I've just hung for Lincoln and it's a bloody aphrodisiac... don't ask me why. I'm weird, I know.

Eddie saunters out with his usual swagger. I love it. I can see the huge, stupid grin that's stretched across his face despite the fact I'm doing everything I can not to look at him, or notice him... or let him think I've noticed him. You'd think this ridiculous little game I've developed for myself would be tiresome by now.

It's not.

Once again, in true Lincoln style, he pulls at me when I'm too busy focusing elsewhere, and I feel the sole of my trainers slip – just a smidge, but before I can even hitch my breath in expectation of a fall, Eddie has his arm on my waist to stop me, grabbing Lincoln's lead rope as he does.

The guys knows what he's doing... I feel the heat immediately. Of course, he doesn't. He has this every day of his life. I wonder how smug he must be at the end of each day, countless women having virtually thrown themselves at him. I will not be one of them. I will, however, enjoy the view and the flirty banter that we have down to a T.

'Thanks,' I mutter as I do my best to turn my instantly reddening face away from him. 'He caught me off guard then.'

'You were too busy watching me I think.' He's deadpan.

'Just making sure you parked in the right space... we all know how crap you are at reversing, don't we? Or would you like me to remind you about Denise's Honda?'

I love our back and forth – the banter and the flirtation. It's honestly what I live for. Does this make me pathetic? Oh God, I'm sad aren't I?

'So how have you been?'

I hate when he starts the small talk. I always wonder whether he's actually bothered at all. He almost throws the comment straight out the side of his mouth, and he does exactly the same now, grabbing Lincoln's back hoof.

'Oh, you know, normal stuff. Work, out with the girls and riding really. Nothing special. You?'

As soon as I say it, I wince internally knowing I've just given him the perfect opportunity to announce his latest conquest. For some reason that escapes my rather logical mind, he enjoys doing this... over and over again. It's not just the thought of him having meaningless sex with someone else that necessarily bothers me, because we're never going to have that sort of relationship. Absolutely not. I mean it. Pretty sure. It's the fact that he might have our kind of rapport with them. When we're good, it's like no one else is on the yard, and I hate the thought of him connecting with someone else like that.

'Same ol' same ol'.'

'So, shagging a million different women each week then?' Why do I even ask? It's like I'm begging him to tell me...

'Why, you jealous?'

'No! Why would I care? I'm just saying, you tell the same old story about the same old blonde every seven weeks. Starting to get a little tiresome, my love.'

'So, what would you prefer, Jen? A story about a sexy, uptight brunette that needs to be shown a good time by a bloke that finally knows what he's doing?'

Well this is bloody different. I swing round and look at him. He looks the same but everything about him tells me there's been a shift. He looks almost as nervous as I feel right now. He's never been so upfront before. Yes, we've always teetered on the edge of admitting there's an attraction here, but we've never crossed that line – never even joked about the thought of actually shagging.

I freeze because I'm nothing short of a coward and just look at him for a moment. He's studying my face, and I can feel the heat rising in my cheeks as he takes in every inch of it. My mouth is dry, and I'm stuttering. I can hear myself stuttering. Oh Christ alive, this needs to end.

With nothing in the think tank, I just turn and head into the barn. Making my way through the horse-lined walkway, I hear the sound of metal hitting the concrete, swiftly followed by the sound of a now shoeless hoof. He's following me. What the fuck? He's following me? What's going on with him today?

'Seriously, you go red at *that*? Come on, Jen. We've been flirting for what... two years? We tease each other every seven fucking weeks on the dot and now I actually mention something about taking it further – not even that, just a hint – and you go cold on me?'

I've found my way into Lincoln's stable, my safe place when the bitchiness of the barn gets a little too much. Unfortunately for me, the barriers of my safe haven have been breached and I look up to find him standing at the stable door. His face is a picture of confusion and frustration. How the hell have I just shut down like this?

The hair on the back of my neck stands on end as he takes a cautious step into my safe place. He's not only blocked my way out, but he's closing the distance there is between us. He's nervous too – I can tell from his quick glance both ways along the barn to make sure no one is in earshot. He knows just as well I do, the potential for gossip in a place like this.

I don't know what comes over me – anger, frustration or sheer fear – but I chuck my shavings fork to the side and widen my stance. 'I thought it was just banter. Just harmless flirting, and more to the point, I'm not uptight. Why do you think I'm uptight?'

'Jen, in the two years I've been shoeing your horse, not once have you mentioned a bloke.'

'Maybe I'm into women!'

'Fuck me, are you serious?' His smirk shifts from just visible to all I can see.

'No, I'm not, but you should never assume. Maybe I'm just discreet. Or maybe I'm sick to death of arsehole men?'

'Maybe if you weren't so uptight, you'd open yourself up to meeting a bloke that treats you the way you deserve to be treated...' His tone has totally changed.

The air I'm desperately dragging into my lungs has shifted. He's gone from cocky to inquisitive and I'm unsure how to handle it. All the times I've told myself I'd never be another notch on his bedpost and now, fuck me, he's actually talking about it.

And just as quickly as he changed his tone, it reverts back to normal. It seems Eddie doesn't feel too comfortable either, or am I just looking into this too much? Maybe he's just taking the piss completely and wanted to see how uncomfortable he could make me. Wouldn't be the first time he's done his absolute best to make me cringe and watch my cheeks flush.

The only trouble is, this time, he's gone quiet on me. Usually after he's done his best to make me squirm, the chit-chat returns to normal and we crack on. This time though, he stays quiet. The silence is palpable, yet my mind is doing overtime, filling my head with nonsensical noise.

Despite my brain screaming at me to do something, say something, I don't. The rest of our time is silent, but it's not the comfortable silence we've experienced before. It's heavy, loaded...

As Eddie knocks the last nail into Lincoln's shoe, he drops his foot and shouts, 'Done!' The harshness of his voice knocks me out of my trance-like state and I look at him. 'Can I book in for seven weeks again? Same time as usual?'

'Yeah, if that works for you?'

'Always – you know that.' There's a softness to my voice. I'm wary and I'm worried – wary about saying something that could put us in that godawful position again and worried I won't get another chance to get that moment back. I can't work out exactly how I feel? Do I regret him cornering me like that and taking it that step further or do I regret not taking advantage of it?

Yes, I've told myself for years I'll never be another notch on his bedpost but what if he's not considering me as a notch per se but rather a whole bloody engraving?

I look at him for a few moments. I'm wondering what he's thinking, but he's not catching my eye. He looks pissed off and I feel like the root of it.

'You OK?' Even I can hear the unease in my voice.

'Yeah, all good. Same old same old, eh, Jen?'

'I'll see you in seven weeks then... unless I bump into you at Hogan's?'

We always seem to bump into each other along the high street. It's not a surprise really. We live in the same area; we have a few mutual friends.

'Yeah, just look for that blonde with the big tits and you'll see me close behind.'

I won't lie, the comments stings, and if I'm not mistaken, I physically wince, but I did just completely knock him back... if he'd actually been serious, so I can't really say anything.

I nod my agreement and turn to Lincoln. I slowly undo the quick-release knot in an attempt to gather my thoughts and hear his van door shut behind me. The engine fires and the tyres start across the concrete. He's gone before I have a chance to shift Lincoln and turn him toward his field. I'm gutted, and instead of longing for my next meeting with him, I'm suddenly uncertain about bumping into him and what's going to happen now.

To take my mind off things, I grab my phone from the dash of my car, through my open window, as we pass it on the way to Lincoln's field and hit speed dial one.

Three rings and Liv picks up as normal. 'Hey gorgeous... how's the handsome Eddie?'

'How the hell do you know I've seen him?'

'Oh God, even I have him on my calendar now. I love chatting with you after and watching you deny all knowledge of a mutual attraction. So was it painstakingly obvious to everyone but the two of you again this time? Have you rung me once more to tell me you're not at all interested and you haven't, in fact, imagined his naked arse pinning you to the back stable wall?'

'You sound like you need a shag more than anything, Liv!'

'Yeah, you're right there, I definitely do, but until I can find myself a man mountain like you've got dripping off your every word, I shall live my life vicariously through you.'

'Nice to know. Fancy Hogan's this weekend? I'm in need of a fucking drink.'

'Yes, Friday night? Sounds like you have a lot to talk about...'

'Like you wouldn't believe.'

I hear her gasp, like I've just delivered a wealth of information. I haven't, but Liv knows me better than anyone so a simple admission like that gives her all the ammunition she needs to try to interrogate me. 'Oh you can't leave me like that until bloody Friday, Jen!'

I hang up with a smirk on my face. She's at work. She won't call me back, but she will send me an abusive text for leaving her hanging.

I smile to myself. Liv makes everything better instantly. She turns monumental fuck-ups into learning curves and cringeworthy moments into laugh-out-loud scenarios. She's the only person who's ever made me laugh at myself. She doesn't take life seriously at all, and when I'm with her, neither do I. What she'll make of this, I have no idea but I'd very much like to find out.

TWO

I'VE HAD the week from hell, mostly brought on by myself. I've done the typical female crap of overthinking something I shouldn't and it's driven me insane. Add to that an arsehole of a client who's demanded work two weeks before the set deadline and it rounded off nicely for me.

I love my job. I love writing, I love being creative and I love the freedom of working from home. I have all the perks of working for a large company, like the contacts and opportunities that come with such big organisations, but I get the relaxed atmosphere of home. I also get to escape that feeling of being a packed sardine on the London Underground, which pleases me more than anyone will ever know. I have a meeting that I've spent most of the day prepping for, but come 3 p.m. and I'm ready to sign off a little early, as I always do Fridays, to start getting ready to meet Liv.

I jump out of the shower, after washing away the stress of that aforementioned arsehole client, and grab my phone as I wander the landing from the shower to my bedroom. It takes about two long strides and I'm there. My flat isn't the biggest place in the world, but I love it, more than anything.

It's super modern and minimalist –maybe a little too modern for my liking – and it's so bloody small, but it's all mine and every time I'm here, I'm proud as punch that I managed to buy it all by myself.

One glance at my bed and I huff, grabbing my riding leggings with my free hand. The wings on the knees are now stained with remnants of the arena from a rather excitable lunging session I gave Lincoln, so I toss them in my washing basket, and as I do, I feel the familiar ping of the phone in my other hand. I've been looking forward to tonight for what feels like bloody ages so I expect to see Liv's name flash up.

But when I glance at the screen, I feel my body flush with heat and that familiar sound of my pulse racing in my hears. Eddie's name fills my vision. Why is he messaging me? We have the next date for Lincoln already in the diary...

I shake the totally unnecessary anxiety that's now filled my head with a quick shudder and pull the phone closer. He's messaged before when he's had a hospital appointment or something like that, so he's obviously just rearranging our next shoeing session. I feel a sense of relief wash over me. Whether it's real or imaginary is anyone's guess, but I press my thumb on the screen anyway, waiting for it to recognise my thumbprint. The usual clicks sound and my messages are opened up before me. He's not messaging about the appointment. Fuck.

EDDIE: Are you meeting Liv in Hogan's tonight?

. . .

I HOVER over the digital keys. Jesus, what the hell do I say? He's never asked before? We just bump into each other and that's it? Why's he suddenly asking?

Shit, he's typing more. He can see that I'm reading this. Fuck this instant message shite.

EDDIE: Does it really take you that long to figure out what to reply? I thought you weren't uptight?

I BLINK AT THE SCREEN. I blink again. My mind is still blank. I think about Liv and know that if I don't reply, she'll bollock me completely for being the wet blanket that I am and consider it extra fodder to discuss when I see her at Hogan's. Hopefully in the same seat as usual.

JEN: Yeah, meeting her in about an hour. Why's that? Hoping to avoid me or want to make sure I catch you with the blonde as soon as I walk in?

I'M a little taken aback by my own confidence. It's oozing in that text but I'm certain it's nowhere to be found here in my bedroom. Where the bloody hell did that come from?

EDDIE: Just checking whether I should wear my farriery uniform as that seems to repel you really easily but don't want to risk putting off one of the usuals...

· · ·

I SIGH, my body slumping as relief washes over me. I feel a huge weight instantly lift from my shoulders that he's talking to me normally, but at the same time, I can't quite shake the feeling of what I think may be disappointment. Am I hoping for something to actually happen? I've always been adamant that I didn't want that so why am I thinking differently now?

I throw my phone on the bed and with a new sense of calmness, I start getting ready. God, I need this night out. Liv will go crazy with the gossip, if you can actually call it that. It's going to be a good night – I can feel it already.

It takes me less than thirty minutes to get ready. I'm a pretty basic dresser, though Liv is a fashionista through and through and I can guarantee she'll have the latest offering from whatever online store is currently on trend. The only trend I've ever embraced is my Vivendi leggings. Anything else is either from the high street or something I've grabbed when I've been forced to go shopping. I'm your typical 'jeans and a nice top' kind of girl and I like it that way. Liv knows me too well by now, but it never stops her from uttering her usual opening line – 'So you dressed up for the occasion then?'

I spot her with ease through a sea of teenagers. I can see her red hair a mile off.

'Liv.' My words barely travel a few feet in front of me between the music and the myriad of voices surrounding me. Thankfully, the combination of my height and heels means Liv spots me quickly. I see her break out into a huge smile, swiftly followed by a frantic wave and some exaggerated pointing. As if I didn't know I was supposed to get to her! She gets there early and grabs the seats – it's the same every time. The thought of walking into a bar on my own just fills me with dread. Put me in a meeting room with a potential client to wow and I'm in my element, but put me in a bar full of strangers and my confidence drops to zero. Liv couldn't be more different – she excels in situations like these, her confidence just oozing, and right now's a prime example.

As I push my way through the crowds, I see her chatting with the people seated next to our usual table. She's made friends already.

My grin gets bigger with every foot closer I get to my best friend. She makes me happy whenever I'm with her, and right now, that's exactly what I need.

'Right, come on, girl, let it all out. Rip the bandage off. Spill it. Tell me every last detail and I promise to tell you whether you're a total cock or not.'

'Cheers, Liv, exactly what I needed. I think I'm likely to need some fuel for this one first,' I admit before catching a glance of what's already on our table.

'Already thought of that, didn't I?' comes screeching out of her mouth as she grabs the bottle, whips it out of the ice and starts pouring.

'Perfect, although I haven't eaten and bubbles always gets me hammered.'

'I might get some better details out of you then... come on, love.'

Glancing around me, looking for no one in particular while knowing full well who I'm looking for, I make sure the coast is clear before launching into a full-on verbal purge of everything that happened at the yard as well as this evening's text messages.

As planned, we spend the night dissecting every single aspect of what happened, what it could mean, what I think it means as well as what it actually means through the eyes of Liv. Liv always cuts straight to the chase, regardless of whether it's going to offend and tells me what I need to hear.

'Let's be honest, love, you were so fucked up with how your stepdad left your mum that you see every bloke as a serial shagger who's only going to leave you as soon as he's got his leg over. I like Eddie, I really do. Will he be another bloke who fucks off as soon as you've bumped uglies? Possibly. But you won't know that until you actually give things a go. Women are no better, you know – trust me, I've been there. They're just as fucked up as the male species.'

I sigh outwardly. She sees me do so, and I look at my feet as her face drops in frustration.

'You can't be single forever, Jen. Men aren't to be hated or feared, for fuck's sake. They can be good bloody fun and despite what happened to your mum' – her hands come up in defence to stop me saying anything – 'despite what happened to her, it's not the be all and end all. Your mum's enjoying a dating life – so can you. You never know, he might end up being a top bloke who'll take you off my hands finally.'

'Oh come on, Liv, as if you could be without me and my constant need for advice on anything that isn't related to work or Lincoln.'

'How is the big brute anyway?' Liv has never been into horses; she's not an animal person in the slightest. She hates the smell, the sounds, even the sheer size of them. But she's a good friend and pretends to be interested in the only real man in my life.

'He's dreamy.' That's an understatement. He's actually sent from the gods and reminds me of that on a daily basis, just standing there in all his grey godliness, looking absolutely bloody stunning.

Before I have a chance to go on, her eyebrows rise so fast

I think they're going to exit her forehead. I spin so quick I crick my neck, but not before I see what's causing her alarm.

Him. He's here. And he's looking at us.

I remove my hand from my now sprained neck in a bid to look remotely relaxed and send him a nod and a wave. Both look and feel utterly pathetic but it's all I can think to do as my pulse quickens and my body temperature rises.

I don't know why it always surprises me but it does, seeing him in anything other than his farriery clothes. It's so strange to see him looking clean. I wonder inwardly whether he smells as clean.

But my thoughts are stopped in their tracks as I notice him cock his head at me and give me a smirk. I'm bloody staring at him. Fuck me, what are you doing, Jen?

I shrug at him and laugh before mentally abusing myself for looking like a complete twat and turn back to Liv, knowing full well I'm about to get a verbal clout.

'I don't want to hear it.'

'Well you bloody will. What the fuck was that? You stared at him like he was some great prize and made your-self look like a complete moron. He's really got you all a quiver, hasn't he? I've never seen you like this, Jen. I think I like it.' And she laughs with enough vigour for the both of us. At least I've been entertaining. She can't say her nights with me are boring, that's for sure.

The hairs on the back of my neck stand on end and I'm suddenly feeling hot again. Before I look to find out what's caused the sudden change in my surroundings, I feel his breath on my ear. I look toward Liv, who's doing her best to look away and mingle with her previous friends.

'You look at me like that down the yard, you know. I often wonder whether you're mentally undressing me or just saving the image so you can enjoy it somewhere a little more private later on. Which one is it?'

I swivel in my chair so I can face him. Him leaning over my shoulder, feeling his breath on my ears and my neck is just too much. I need to break the connection until I know for sure what this is or, at the very least, what I want this to be.

I cough and splutter as I turn my body and he shifts his so my legs are suddenly straddling his waist. I knew he was tall but right now, despite me being sat on a pretty high bar stool, he's still towering over me. He inches further toward me, closing the gap between us so my legs are now tight on his hips. My nostrils are filled with a masculine scent. If I had to hazard a guess, I'd say Jo Malone of some description. It's woody, yet through it all, I still get a hint of smoke and it fills my head.

I lean back, just to bring him back into my field of vision, and as I do, he leans into me, holding my eye contact as he places his pint on the table behind me. He leans in just close enough that I feel his breath on me. But it's his intense stare that takes my focus. I hold eye contact for longer than feels comfortable and breathe him in, begging for some of my usual sharp tongue to return to me. But it's lost. All of it.

'Been talking about me, have you?'

'No, not really. You may have sprung up when I was telling Liv about Lincoln – that was about it.' My nerves are still getting the best of me.

'Why didn't you reply to my text?'

'Thought it was a rhetorical question.' And I'm back.

He falters slightly before leaning in. 'You're right, it was a rhetorical question because the answer's bloody obvious, isn't it?'

I stare straight at him, waiting for the perfect retort to come to me, but it doesn't. My mind is filled only with him – with the heat I feel from having his skin so close to mine. I feel the hairs on his forearm and see the stubble already coming through from what must be a recent shave. My eyes devour his entire face, and as they do I see him bite his lip. Watching his teeth sink into his plump bottom lip does things to me I'd rather not admit, but I can't ignore the sudden throbbing between my legs.

Just as I think I'm about to do something to ease my desire, to change whatever this is between us, I hear a voice and it's not Liv. 'What do we have here, eh? You two look a little close.'

Eddie cocks his head to the side, and as he does I feel his long, dark curls tickle the side of my face. As soon as he realises who it is, he stands upright and takes a step back. 'Angel, nice to see you. How's Roman?'

'He's good, all the better for seeing you yesterday. You know your magic hands keep us all feeling good.'

I feel her glance my way as she says it. The rumours about Eddie and Angel have been floating around for years, but I've never believed them. Mostly down to the age differ-ence, though it may simply be because I'd rather not believe it. She's beautiful, petite, but she's also fairly young in my eyes – a young woman with a kid's arsey attitude. The problem is, her older brothers are known throughout the town as being quite the menacing double act, which I think has inflated her ego more than it needs. Despite the age gap between her and Eddie, I see a connection between them. Maybe the word connection is wrong, but there's definitely something between them. A secret almost that ties them together, but it seems no matter how catty this young woman gets, he never says a thing.

It's like Eddie can feel my deflation, or more than likely see it, as he shouts, 'I was just admiring this goddess. How fit does Jen look out of her yard clothes...' He trails off, staring at me before he stutters, 'Well, I mean in different clothes. You know what I mean?' And he cocks his head, looking ever so slightly nervous, though it's not long before his usual cockiness returns with a quick, 'But hey, I wouldn't be adverse to seeing you out of your clothes,' before he shoots me a quick wink.

I melt. I physically fucking melt, yet because of Angel's presence, my sharp tongue has disappeared once more. Fuck.

'How have you been, Angel?' I asked, hoping my utter distain for her doesn't show in my tone.

The fact that I don't like her could easily be mistaken for jealousy, but it's not. It's plain and simple hatred of the lowest form. I hate her. Harsh? Yes. Fair? Absolutely. She's the bitchiest cow on the yard. If your saddle pad doesn't match your riding clothes then you're scum in her eyes. She enjoys Daddy's credit card a little too much and looks down on anyone who's anything but pristine in her eyes.

The pitfalls of being on a livery yard. The equestrian sport, as much as I love it, has to be one of the bitchiest environments I've ever been in, but I just love my boy so much. I dream of the day that I can own my own little parcel of land and have Lincoln and another horse together, just the two of them on our own private little plot. One day it might happen. If I win the lottery. Until then, I have to put up with people like Angel putting me down for the way I care for my horse, the fact he isn't always in an outline and the fact that sometimes, just sometimes, I allow him to get a little muddy. What a choker.

As always, I'm treated to a full body visual as she steps

back, almost presenting herself to what she must feel is her competition. Red soles on the shoes, very expensive. A tight bandeau dress to show off her 'natural' curves. Yes, yes. Meow. And her hair and make-up are, as usual, pristine. I suddenly feel entirely inadequate. Her move has worked wonders.

'I'm great, my little love. As always. We're out this weekend competing at a PSG. That means Prix St Georges.' She quite clearly slows her words down as if I'm unaware what the letters PSG stands for.

'Yes. I'm well aware of what PSG means within the realms of dressage. Can't say I'm a fan of it myself. Always seemed a cop-out for people who were too scared to jump, but what do I know?'

I'm awarded a slap on the arm by Liv, reminding me to curb the bitching. She knows I'll only hate myself for it tomorrow. I don't actually mean it. I'm quite fond of a little dressage, but I know that Angel's too scared to jump thanks to an accident she had years back when we used to be friends. Back before she turned into a complete twat, I should say. So it feels like the only way to stick the knife in.

I won't lie that I get a little kick out of the half smile I see creep over Eddie's face at my quip, though I still try my best to offer a much nicer, much more Jen-style olive branch so to speak. 'I'm sure you'll do well. You and Roman are quite the team. I'd like to come watch actually. See what it's all about, this stress-age they all talk about.'

'I don't think it's for you,' is quickly fired back as she takes another look at what I'm wearing before my eyes begin to burn at the sight of her running her hand up and down Eddie's arm.

This is all beginning to feel like a pathetic playground fight over a boy. It's a fight I'm not prepared to have and the feeling of sheer 'ick' – if that's even a word – reminds me exactly why I didn't want to take things further with Eddie in the first place.

As if by magic, or some mentally connected coconut and string telephone link, Liv grabs my arm. 'Sorry to break up this lovely little social, but Jen and I have somewhere to be. Come on, love.'

I'm pulled from my seat and thrown a sideways glance. 'Yes, Liv and I have dinner reservations. Have a great night, guys.'

Before I can make it down the step to head toward the door, Eddie grabs my hand. Electricity shoots through me like lightning and it's all I can do to try to avoid him.

His body shoots round me as he places himself at my eye level. 'Jen, we were talking?'

My attempt at sounding sincere fails me completely. 'Yeah, I know, I forgot we've got plans. But Angel's here now. You guys will have a great evening I'm sure.'

He leans in further, gripping my hand tighter and gently pulling my other wrist from Liv's grasp. His mouth touches my ear and I feel his alcohol-stained breath as he whispers, 'I don't want to enjoy an evening with Angel. I came here to see you, Jen, and you know I did.'

'Sorry, gotta go. But I'll see you at the yard in a few weeks or something. Have fun, guys.' And I turn as quickly as I can, determination racing through me as I desperately try to remind myself why I'm leaving and not taking this further like the throb between my legs desperately wants me to.

There's a reason I've avoided this for so long and it's for shit like this. I don't have time to be fighting off pathetic girls who all want a slice of the hot farrier. Yes, he's hot. Fuck me, he's hot, but Christ, if it's going to cause this every time I leave the house or bump into someone around the yard, then fuck that.

The gossip too, that would be never-ending. I'd constantly be regaled with ~~tails~~ TALES of him flirting with this livery or that livery, or informed of his flirtatious chit-chat at another yard. It would drive me insane. No. I've made up my mind. However much I'd love to jump his bones right now, it's just not happening. He'd only want to fuck for a while and then he'd move on to the next girl. He's a farrier – that's what they all do, right? We do it all the time with men: we always think we're going to be the one to change them and it never happens. It would be no different with him.

THREE

SEVEN WEEKS HAVE PASSED. Albeit rather slowly but they've passed. Usually I'd be wishing the time away until my next farrier visit, the appointment screaming at me from my diary day in and day out, but this time it's different. This time he's ignored me every time he's been on the yard dealing with other horses. I've had the odd nod but that's it. I suppose he's angry with me. He must feel like I've rejected him, but surely he realises that it's for the best.

My anxiety has gone up several notches, every single time I've seen him and he's treated me like a stranger on the street. I've spent hours upon hours wondering what the fuck I'll say to him when he comes to see Lincoln and now it's time.

Instead of being mentally prepared to throw a few humorous one-liners his way, get him laughing and try to wrestle back some sense of normality between us, I'm stressed to my eyeballs and surprisingly enough it's nothing to do with him.

I've had a deadline looming and I'm no closer to finishing the piece than when I started it two weeks ago.

This is the first time in my writing career that I've stumbled, that I've dealt with the so-far-elusive writer's block, and I don't know what to do. I have a suspicion that this situation with Eddie has affected me more than I'd like to admit but I'll never own up to that. Not even to myself.

Liv has been the best friend as always and messaged me this morning, telling me to stay calm and just be my normal self. Apparently my current state of sweaty and flustered wouldn't work, so I was promptly instructed to be a cooler version of the shipwreck I'd somehow turned in to. That comment was ~~dually~~ *DULY* noted and then she was swiftly told to fuck off. Which she did actually. I thought she'd take a little more persuading, but perhaps she's aware of just how shitty I'm feeling with Eddie, work and actually having to face it all today.

I'd thought of a variety of different things to say, ranging from funny to serious and everything in between, and I'd changed my mind on my opening line about seven. Thousand. Times. In those moments when the doubt would creep in and my heart would win the battle with my head, I'd wondered whether or not to push it with him. Today I'm thinking that exact thing as I watch him pull into the yard, heading for his usual spot.

Should I just push it further? Should I tell him I want to kiss him? That I can't stop thinking about the feelings he stirred up inside of me when he leant across me and brushed my skin. That I can't stop thinking of him every time I touch myself. He's the first thing I think about when I wake up and yup, you guessed it, the last thing I think about when I go to sleep. That I'm currently struggling to work because his eyes, his gorgeous dark curls and his thick forearms have stolen every word from my vocabulary and made it virtually impossible to think of anything else?

Or should I take the sensible route, not the easy route, because now this is hard as fuck. The sensible route ensures I still have a good relationship with my farrier and I'm no one's gossip fodder.

I'm quickly distracted from my tumbling thoughts as I'm nudged by Lincoln. He knows my mind's elsewhere and also that it's time for him to dive into the huge net of haylage I have in my hands.

'You're looking a little lean you know, Linc. More than I'd like. I know we're coming into spring but I'd prefer you a bit plumper so you're going to be moving on to haylage completely now. I might chuck in another small net of hay so you don't get bored, but you need a few more calories.'

He looks at me blankly. He knows what I mean. I'm almost sure of it.

I throw his headcollar on and link the lead rope to the bottom ring, then half smile at the familiar sound of Eddie's shoes hitting the concrete as we walk through the barn, before I'm hit with his gravelly tone. 'Earth to Jen. Where are you in that head of yours?'

His voice brings me out of what must have been a trance-like state because I have no idea how he managed to park up and get his chaps on ready for Lincoln in that short space of time.

I stare at him blankly for a few seconds before lifting my eyes to the sky and taking note of the birds circling ahead. 'Hey,' I murmur and lower my eyes to meet his.

Deadly. Just fucking deadly.

Grabbing the worn net, I lift the haylage up and start tying it, staring dead at the wall.

Think, Jen! For Christ sake think of something to say!

'How have you been?'

Smooth, Jen, real smooth. My eye roll is severe but thankfully I'm still staring at the wall.

'What are you staring at?'

'What?' I virtually shout at him, almost feeling like I've been caught off guard despite my weeks and weeks of planning this exact moment.

'What are you staring at? You look like you've lost a few marbles just staring at the wall? What are you admiring? The brickwork? The fascia boards or what?

'I... I don't actually know, you know? Something must have caught my eye.'

Just like that, the first exchange of awkward small talk is done and dusted, and instead of feeling broken and filled with awkward silences, it flowed as usual. More than I thought it would. It almost felt like normal. Is this a good thing or a bad thing, because right now I'm not actually sure?

I have the sudden feeling of everything simply being brushed under the carpet and I don't like it. Usually that's my favourite feeling. I don't have to deal with things and they can simply be... forgotten. But this time, it's left me feeling uncertain and most definitely unhappy. For fuck's sake, what do I want? The great big, whacking pink elephant in the barn has been pushed aside and replaced with a fidgety Lincoln. But my unease, this deep-seated feeling of something being not quite right, just won't leave.

With Lincoln in place and Eddie beginning his usual routine, I find myself feeling downtrodden. Without asking, I walk the long and somewhat lonely walkway through the empty barn to the tea station and flick the switch for the kettle. Grabbing two dusty mugs, I run them under the tap then chuck them down in front of the now-steaming kettle. Tea makes everything better, right?

One of the mugs has a crack along the rim. With the way I threw it down, I could have sworn it grew an extra few millimetres. It mirrors the cracks I feel are beginning to show every time I come close to Eddie – what was the crack of a smile and what now feels like a crack within my heart. I was always teased for being too icy during my teen years. Maybe they were right?

'You never give a bloke a chance Jen!' or 'Come on, stop being such a cow' were all-too-familiar remarks during my weekends clubbing. I just figured I'd grow out of it at some point or, at the very least, meet a guy that saw through it, but right now I'm not so sure.

Without realising it, I've thrown a teabag in each cup, poured in the milk (yes first – that's how I like it) and filled both cups with boiling water. I make a grab for the grubby spoon and start stirring when a hand grabs my wrist and stops it dead in its tracks.

I glance at the rough skin on the hand. You can see the hours of work he puts in, day in, day out. Whether it's ice cold out, sodden with rain or searingly hot, he's out there working, and I admire him for it.

I run my gaze along his arm and up to his face, my breathing mirroring the million miles an hour my mind is currently racing at. I feel like a prey animal who's seen the predator that's about to take its first bite, and I'm not sure if I want it to be over quickly, or for him to take it real slow.

'Stir it any longer and the spoon's going to melt...'

I say nothing – just continue looking at him. He keeps his hand on my wrist and I don't shake him off; I just look at it like something that once felt alien has happened but now feels completely right – as if his hand should always have been there. I've always heard people say silence is deafening and right now the silence is screaming at me.

His breathing. My breathing. The awkward shift of the spoon as he lifts my wrist to take it from me with his other hand, which has come from nowhere and is suddenly reaching around my waist. I can feel his entire body standing behind me, up against my liquid insides.

My gaze darts from his hands to his lips and back to his hands. I bite my lip to stop myself from making the stupid, incoherent sounds that are racing through my mind and feel a warmth rise through me. I close my eyes for what feels like a split second, focusing on the redness in my cheeks, trying anything to make it just go away. Surely I can't be the only one feeling this?

That question is quickly answered when I feel him swallow behind me, his body shifting. I feel him widen his stance, steady himself almost, before he falters, as if he meant to say something and then thought better of it. Definitely not just me.

As stunned as I currently feel, I can't resist my body's own need to take him all in, and I look over my shoulder before turning my whole body around. Except his doesn't move. He keeps his same stance and the exact same closeness, making me physically contort so I have to support myself by placing my one free hand behind me on the tea station.

I see the cogs turning, his eyes darting from my lips to my eyes and back again. It's almost like he's having an internal conversation. Should he kiss me? Should he walk away? Is he trying to talk himself into it or out of it?

He drops my wrist and then glides both hands up my arms, tugging on the one suddenly gripping the table behind me like a vice. As my hand is removed or I let go – I'm not entirely sure what happens in all honesty as my concentration is focused solely on his face – I'm manoeuvred to the bars outside of Lincoln's stable.

It's silent still, the only sound being our breathing, and I'm sure I see him shake his head. It's only slight but he definitely did it. Then he lowers his head toward me, and as he does, I let mine fall back, almost inviting him in. It's automatic, like my body responds to his presence unconsciously. My eyes naturally close and I wait, lips parted, ready to feel his on mine – but I don't.

I open my eyes and see him staring at me again. He's thinking again, but what the bloody hell is he thinking? We've already ventured past the point of no return, and if anything, not kissing me would be a lot more awkward. 'What's going on?'

'Just be quiet, Jen.' And with that he kisses me. He lingers for a moment, his nose touching mine as he searches for my lips, holding eye contact before his mouth meets mine. The sense of urgency I was expecting isn't there. It's soft. Tender even.

His lips are swiftly followed by the rest of his body as he presses his chest, stomach and groin up against me. He's having to bend at the knee to meet me, but his body engulfs me, physically and mentally, and his scent is intoxicating – soaked hay and farrier smoke lingering in the air as his lips push harder. His tongue entices mine to join his, and as it does my wrists leave the constraint of his hold and then my hands are in his hair. I'm holding on tight, pushing him harder into me. My world is suddenly consumed by him, desperate for as much as I can get.

As I push up on my tiptoes in a desperate attempt to get more of him, if that were possible, his kiss, which have become more urgent with the help of my vice-like grip in his hair, slows once more. He bites my lip and then tugs on it as his body peels away from mine.

I feel the emptiness almost immediately – the heat between us, the wetness between my legs begging for the solid feeling of his erection, which had been pushing against me through his jeans. Instead, I'm leaning against the bars looking misplaced. He steps back, takes one more look at me and then turns on his heels – just like that he's walking out of the barn, shouting over his shoulder, 'Lincoln's done. I'll see you next time.'

I stand there, stunned. There's no other word for it.

My fingers lift and touch my lips, as if to check whether he was really there. They're sizzling.

I watch him throw his tools in the back of his truck and then slam the door. Hard enough to make my usually bombproof Lincoln look up from his haynet.

With the sound of the engine, the truck sings into life and he's gone.

I'm still standing by the tea station. Two cups of tea stand next to the now-cooling kettle, yet my body is as hot as it's ever been. I have no fucking clue what's just happened, but what I do know is that I want it again. Scratch that, I *need* it again. How the fuck do I get it?

FOUR

I SPEND the next ten minutes mucking out. Lincoln's stall is the only place I have the mental capacity to make big life decisions but nothing comes to me. I skip out, shift Lincoln's old nets and dump what needs to be thrown on the muck heap, then grab a new bale of wood chip and empty it into his stall, ensuring it's a foot deep as usual and piling on the banks as I normally do. I square it all off with the back of my shavings fork and then head to the feed room to start filling two nets for the night. He gets one of haylage and one of hay. Still nothing comes to me. Nothing makes sense at the moment. It's just fucking weird. Why kiss me and then instantly act like it didn't happen?

I do the only thing I know to do in a situation like this and give Liv a ring.

'What? What's happened?'

'How do you know something's happened?'

'Because I've spent the morning pumping you up, mentally preparing you for meeting the only man who's ever got you this worked up and you call me immediately after. I gather you're not calling me to tell me absolutely nothing so what's bloody happened?'

'He kissed me...' And for the next few minutes I relive every passionate moment with Eddie. I give her every angle. Every word that was said, every tender touch and more before I wait for her usual onslaught of advice, but this time she's silent.

'Well, say something.'

'I'm thinking for Christ's sake, I'm thinking. This has never happened before. You've never let a bloke get to you this much, and more to the bloody point, you've never rung with an actual rundown of your dirty little antics in the barn. I always knew you were a minx.'

'Do I call him?'

'Oh for Christ's sake, it's not 1999. You can call a bloke, and last time I checked you were twenty-six years old for fuck's sake. Don't be so pathetic. Although I wouldn't call him.'

'Great advice, Liv. Fucking top advice. Not confusing at all.' I'm so glad I called her... genuinely. Her ranting is exactly what I need right now – it blocks out the noise in my own head.

I end the call on a promise to speak with her later. She did her best to convince me to head out, but my deadline is calling me so I can't be anywhere other than at my desk as soon as I've finished up here.

I pick up the haynet and head back toward his stall to tie it up, ready for Lincoln as he beds down for the night. He's still munching happily, tied up outside. I catch a quick glance of him, and as I do, I see another car has parked up a little behind him. There's someone else here. Shit! I mentally berate myself for not keeping the conversation with Liv until I was at home. If anyone's heard anything I'll

be the fucking talk of the yard. These women gossip enough
– I don't need to give them anymore fuel.

'So you kissed him then, did you?'

SHIT.

'Sorry?'

Angel looks at me with the usual sweet venom she
boasts and asks again, 'So you kissed him then?'

'I'm not entirely sure what business that is of yours. If
you don't mind, I need to finish off Lincoln. I've gotta get
back to work.'

I have to sidestep her to keep heading toward Lincoln's
stall. She does her best to intimidate me by standing her
ground, not moving even an inch for me. It's noted but
doesn't have the desired effect considering she's a 21-year-
old who's barely finished puberty. What does Eddie see in
her? Oh Christ, she's getting under my skin if I'm already
thinking like this!

I hear her turn on her long black riding boots as she
follows me out.

'I think you made it everyone's business when you were
shouting about it in the barn, love. Oh, it's sweet anyway.
Don't be embarrassed. I know he's always spoken fondly of
you. Said he felt sorry for you because you never seemed to
have any male attention.'

'Angel, I'm not talking about this with you.'

'No, no, I'm not pushing. I'm just saying, I did wonder
when he was going to do something. He's been saying you
need a little attention – that you need a good shag to lighten
you up. This could be the best thing for you. Although I'm
not too sure being a notch on a farrier's bedpost is going to
be enough, but hey, it's a start, right?'

I stop in my tracks, not quite sure how to respond.
Angel is a few years younger than me and loves getting her

way. I guess this answers the question of whether she has feelings for Eddie or not. I look at her, stunned, and lucky me, she carries on.

'He just texted me actually. Said he had something funny to tell me. This must have been it. I'm guessing that's why he left without saying a word.'

'You listened to every word of my conversation? Are you jealous or something, Angel? Is that why you're being this vindictive?'

'Oh don't be silly; I'm just being honest. You know my relationship with Eddie is... special. So stay the fuck away from him, Jen. I'm not into threesomes unless the other one's actually attractive.'

And with that, she walks out, grabbing her horse's head-collar, heading off to her field.

I'm left standing there like a moron, dumbfounded by the sheer audacity that she's displayed.

It's crazy to think that we used to be friends. We were so close, then she fell off her horse and blamed me for it because it was my horse spooking that caused her fall. It wouldn't have been so bad had she not broken her leg, which then led her parents to sell her dressage pony so it didn't go to waste during her recovery. The fact that they'd have made a pretty penny on the gelding didn't seem to enter Angel's mind at the time. Instead, it was all my fault, and of course the scruffy little cob mare I was borrowing at the time.

Ever since then, it's always been pretty icy between us. I've never actively sought friction with her, but if I'm being honest with myself, I've never truly avoided it either, often throwing the odd provocative retort where and when I can.

My mind wanders back to what she said about them having a special relationship and I can't deny the sickly feeling that hits the pit of my stomach. I honestly thought our kiss meant something. Granted, I didn't know what, but I thought it meant *something*.

So it was a pity party thing? A kiss to make me feel better about myself or destroy my self-confidence entirely. That's obviously what they were discussing after I left them in Hogan's.

The feeling of humiliation is outweighed ever so slightly by the sheer disappointment at the situation I've found myself in. I told myself time and again that it would never go further than a few cheeky remarks during his visits, but it did and I loved every second of it. Within seconds, I felt totally overtaken with emotion – the way he made me feel, the way my body reacted to his touch – and now? Now I just feel used. I feel embarrassed, and I feel like a complete moron for falling for it. No wonder he hesitated so much. No wonder he took his time. Because he wasn't interested to begin with, or maybe his conscience was telling him to stop, though he clearly ignored it.

I tie Lincoln's net, throw in his feed bucket and slowly walk him into his stall. Then I sweep up the mess of hoof trimmings and try my hardest to treat it as if I'm sweeping away the mess that Eddie's left in my head and the car crash he's left in my heart.

It invariably doesn't work and I leave the yard, a crumbled mess on the inside but my usual icy exterior firmly back in place.

FIVE

THE REST of the week seems to have flown by in a complete blur. I made my deadline, which I have to say, I'm surprised about. Somehow, and I'm not entirely sure how, I got home with a new determination. Words flowed out of me and I created the best feature I've put out in a long time. It focused on architecture and the use of specialist companies for roof trusses – quite literally the most boring subject I've ever written about – but it gave me a total escape. The client was so happy that he's commissioned another fifteen features, which I'm not entirely sure is a good thing considering I only seem capable of writing this type of content when I'm burning with rage and my heart has been pulverised into a crumpled mess.

Eddie has messaged more times than I can count and I've ignored them all. I have no idea what to say to him. Do I have to get a new farrier now? Where the fuck am I going to get a new farrier from? The waiting lists around here are bloody huge.

I've done my utmost to avoid Angel at the barn too. Yes, a 26-year-old woman is avoiding a 21-year-old, but let's face it, she has the attitude of a fucking Mafia wife and I just don't need the drama right now. Nor do I want to be reminded of Eddie's complete betrayal. Or should that be my complete and utter gullibility? Perhaps both.

This is likely the fifth day in a row that I've paid someone to finish Lincoln off for me. I've been down each morning at 5 a.m. instead of my usual mid-morning visit and poor Lincoln has seemed in complete and utter shock each time. His usual morning routine has been upended. Thankfully, my friend Maggy, who owns a scruffy little Shetland – or Shitland, whatever you like to call them – has let me grab him to turn out with Lincoln, otherwise I'd likely have had to pay someone to turn him out as well.

I must say, I've actually enjoyed the early mornings, and today was no exception. Riding over the brow of the hill just as the sun rises gives you quite the sight, and I must admit it sets me up for the day more than my writing does. Maybe that's why I've been so productive.

I have a meeting with an editor later for the local newspaper, so after riding Lincoln this morning and then knocking out a few more pages for my architecture client, I spend some time preening myself. It's been a while since I've set foot in an office.

I jump out of the tub and wrap my freshly tumble-dried towel around me. It's still warm and fluffy. This is my time to procrastinate. I sit at the end of my bed and zone out as I flick through the channels on my TV as my body dries. I always do this. This is a time when I could be blow-drying my hair, painting my nails – or what's left of my nails – and instead I just sit here. Fluffy towels and ample time before my next appointment is my weakness – I'm certain of it.

I toss the remote onto the bed and clutch the top of my towel to my chest as I finally get my arse in gear and stand up. As I do, the buzzer goes – someone's at the security door. I'm quickly reminded of Eileen at number thirty-two, who was popping to the corner shop for a few bits and asked me to buzz her in so she wouldn't have to worry about her keys. I buzz her in, picturing her faffing with her bags and the door handle, and wonder whether or not I should run down in my towel, but think twice. The last time I did, she almost had a heart attack at the amount of skin on show. Instead I make an about-turn back to my bedroom.

I sling a few pairs of jeans on the bed and wonder whether I can get away with wearing a ripped jean with my Louboutins? It's the media industry after all, so it's unlikely everyone's going to be in suits.

Then I hear a knock at the door. Bloody hell. She's climbed those stairs quick. Unless it's not her.

I tiptoe to the door wondering who the fuck I've just let through the security door, cursing myself yet again for my fucking laziness and stupidity. I lean on the door, desperate not to make a sound and look through the peephole.

Fuck me, there he is!

'Jen, open the door.'

I can hear the desperation in his voice. It would usually work, but the anger in me is starting to drown him out, swiftly followed by the humiliation. I hear Angel's words in my head over and over again and suddenly want to throttle him.

'Just wait a second,' I shout over my shoulder as I run to my bedroom to grab something to put on that doesn't threaten to expose every inch of my body to him.

I grab my ripped jeans and my flip-flops, then throw on a bra. I'm tussling with a vest top as I open the door. Let him have a peek at what he's never fucking touching again.

'What do you want?'

'What's with the attitude? And why the fuck are you ignoring every single one of my messages? Is it because I walked out? I didn't mean to, Jen, I just—'

'Oh fucking save it!' Stepping backwards, I head back across the hall and move into the kitchen. I may have just let him in, but I'm determined to not only stand my ground but also give him more than a piece of my mind. The steam is virtually blowing out of my ears right now, but I'm in my place, my home. This is my territory.

I hear him follow me in and the door slam behind me. 'Angel told me everything, you know. Your little discussion in Hogan's after I left.'

'Jen girl, I'm lost?'

'Yeah, of course you are. You have no idea. I know you're friends with her older brothers; I know you're close with her. The rumours about you two flew around for years, but I never for one second thought you talked about me like that with her. You've made me look like a complete fool.'

'There's nothing going on with me and Angel. Yes, I'm friends with her brothers, so I have to be courteous to her. But that's it, and let me make one thing perfectly clear, I *never* fucking said anything about you to her when you walked out on me.'

'Walked out on you? Are you kidding? It was either that or sit there and catfight over you with a fucking child.'

He steps toward me and I instinctively step back. I need the space for the simple fact that his presence is doing things to me that I'd rather it didn't.

'I asked you to stay.' The frustration is clear on his face as he takes another step toward me, closing the gap thanks to the worktop at my back.

I place my hands behind me to steady myself and broaden my stance some more then watch as he gives my entire body a once-over. I instantly feel heat between my thighs. How after everything he and that shitty little bitch have done does my body still want him? It's like it's betraying me.

He must sense it, as he moves in closer, closing the distance to a final few inches.

His huge, rough hands send sparks through me as he lightly touches my upper arm. A slightly confused look washes over his face, as if he's having a battle with himself, and I voice my thoughts without even thinking. 'You look like you're physically struggling to go against what your head is telling you. If it's this difficult then it's obviously not right for you, and in all honesty, I'd rather not get caught up in whatever the fuck this is, because I'm the one who's going to get hurt.'

'Do you honestly think I'd hurt you?' Not only does he ask me this with words but his eyes are pleading with me too. He's wounded at the sheer thought.

His hand rises from my arm to cup the side of my face, the other steadying himself as he places it on the worktop in between my body and my other hand. We're as close as we can be without our bodies being intertwined and the tension is palpable.

'Jen, I could never hurt you. Surely you know that by now?'

'Then what's all this shit with Angel?'

'It's complicated.'

'How?'

'Do we really need to talk about it now?'

'Yes, she made me feel like utter shite and from what I've heard has the entire fucking yard discussing my pathetic crush on you, the pitying farrier who's desperate to get out my clutches...'

'You have a crush on me?' His face breaks into a half smile, and I squeeze my eyes and pinch the bridge of my nose in total exasperation.

'That's what you got from all of that? You're a typical fucking bloke aren't y—' But before I can finish my sentence, his lips crash into mine with a force stronger than his farrier's hammer.

If our last kiss was tender and loving, this is the complete opposite – animalistic and carnal. Our breathing is heavy and laboured as we struggle to catch our breath amongst the physical grappling we seem to be doing, our tongues smashing together, desperate for more, but we physically can't give any more than we already are.

His hands leave my face and the worktop and he pulls my backside away from the counter so he can slide them onto each cheek, gripping with a force I've never felt before. The pain of his grip sends waves of pleasure through me and my head falls back in response.

He takes the invitation with ease, leaving his exploration of my mouth to bite my neck. As he does, he squeezes my backside once more and lifts me up onto the worktop so I'm level with him, then moves one hand up to grip my waist and the other to pull my bra cup down, revealing one breast. He immediately bites down on my nipple and begins to suck as my hands meet his thick mop of hair, pulling him even closer, if that were possible. I pin him so tightly against my tit that I wonder for a second how he could possibly be breathing.

His other hand moves to my other breast, pulling the second cup down to reveal all of me. I reach down as he squeezes both breasts and feel his rock-hard erection underneath his jeans. Even from here I can tell he's huge.

'Too many clothes, Jen; there's too many clothes' he

pants as he moves between my breasts and back again. He's pulling my bra straps and my vest straps down my arms, almost pinning them in before I rip my arms up and out in search of freedom. In search of him.

My breasts are exposed completely, my top and bra hanging around my waist, but it's not enough. There's still too much between us.

I grapple with his belt and almost rip it from his jeans before unbuttoning and unzipping his fly. I struggle to pull his jeans down over his erection, but frustration gets the better of him as he leaves me momentarily to rip them down.

His cock is long and thick and wet. He's desperate for me, his body getting itself ready for me just as much as I am for him.

He pulls at my jeans, unbuttoning them faster than it took me to do them up and curls one arm around my waist, lifting me away from the worktop. As he does, his other hand pulls them down, taking my knickers with them.

I kick them off, along with my flip-flops, as he slaps me back down on to the worktop, but instead of hearing them hit the floor, all I hear his him, breathing into me as he attacks my mouth once more. I grab the hem of his T-shirt, lifting it over his head, denying his lips the taste of mine just for a split second, but it's enough to earn me a growl from his now angry face.

Seeing him desperate to touch me, to have me, is intoxicating enough, but actually feeling him on me consumes me more than I ever thought it could.

He knees my legs apart and puts his hand down straight onto my soaking-wet opening, rubbing my clit with expert precision, as if he knows every inch of my body already. Oh. My. God. He knows what's he's doing,

'You like that, baby, don't you? You're so fucking wet.'

All I can do is moan in response. And he plays with me, teasing me, bringing me to the edge then stopping. Leaving my build-up to die down before he ventures back.

The pure eroticism I'm feeling with his thick, hard cock in my hand, pumping his shaft up and down as he plays with my wetness, is like nothing else, but it's not enough – I still can't be sated. I need him inside me and I need him inside me now.

It's like he reads my mind as he grips my arse cheeks, leaving my wet pussy feeling exposed and wanting without his hands, and pulls me to the edge of the worktop, but I needn't have worried – I don't wait for long.

With a deep and delicious growl, he enters me, pushing me wider than I thought possible.

'Oh fuck,' escapes me and he stops, easing his penetration to give me more time to get used it.

'You OK? That OK? Fuck, Jen, speak; I'm struggling to hold back here...'

He lowers his gaze and pulls my face up to meet his, but my eyes are closed. 'Open your eyes – I need to see you.'

And I do – they flip open in immediate response, registering the sheer desire that's written all over this face. He pumps into me harder and harder, grunting on each one thrust as I scream, struggling to take him all but desperate for more. I feel myself building again as his thumb heads back and begins working my already worked-up clit. The heat travels through my body. 'I'm getting close; I'm getting fucking close.'

'Me too, I'm nearly fucking there. Jesus, how do you get me this worked up. Fuck.'

'Don't stop. Don't stop. Please don't stop.' And just like that I crumble as the vibrations of what can only be described as a vicious orgasm take over my entire body. I ripple, I crumple before him as he growls, letting me know he's cum too, and just like that, his thrusts slow and he leans into me, sweaty and panting into my neck.

Oh shit. His rasp has gained another notch.

SIX

I'M NOT sure how I currently feel, apart from deeply satisfied after having one of the most powerful orgasms of my life. I can't look at him for a second because despite how amazing it was, it still doesn't erase the fact that Angel said what she did and I could very well have just played straight into a rather wicked game.

Despite what's been said, my gut feeling is there's something more to this and Eddie isn't telling me the whole story, though to be fair, he's not telling me anything.

I slide down from the worktop and squeeze past him. He cocks his head and tries to make eye contact as I leave, but I avoid his gaze and take myself to the bathroom to clean up before heading to my bedroom to grab another pair of jeans and a fresh bra and top. One that doesn't smell of sex – which the ones hanging around my waist very much do.

'You OK?' He appears at my bedroom door, leaning against the frame as he buttons up his jeans.

'Yeah, I have a meeting in the high street. I've got to get ready and make a move.'

'Can I see you tonight?'

'Only if you want to tell me what the fuck is going on?'

I didn't mean for that to sound as harsh as it obviously did from the way his body sags and his head lowers.

'There's nothing going on between me and Angel, but I think the most important question right now is whether you're on a contraceptive or not?'

'Yes, you're fine. I'm more concerned about whether you've caught anything from all the notches?' I mumble as I dive deeper into my wardrobe.

'Notches? What's that mean?'

'In your own time, Ed.'

'Ahhh I see.'

I watch him out the corner of my eye as he wanders further into the bedroom. He comes to a halt behind me and places his hands on my shoulders. 'You want to know if I've been shagging around, whether I'm still shagging around or whether I only want to shag around with you. That's what you mean?'

'Eddie, I didn't propose. I'm not asking you to be my boyfriend, for fuck's sake. This isn't an American teen drama where I undo my scruffy plait, whip off my glasses and ta da, I'm a stunning model you instantly fall in love with. I'm just concerned about my health after that fucking stupid mistake in there.'

I flinch at my own words, as does he. I bolt around to look at him, desperate to reassure him that's not what I meant. 'That came out wrong.'

'Yeah, don't worry.' He's heading to the door and out toward the kitchen, with me following swiftly behind.

'Ed, for fuck's sake, I didn't mean the shag was a mistake; I meant not using a condom. That was a mistake.'

'Yes, because I'm a farrier who must shag every fucking woman he comes into contact with. I must be fucking riddled, eh? Don't worry – I know exactly what you mean, and for what it's worth, I thought it was more than a shag or a quick fuck, but my mistake.'

How on earth have the tables turned on me? Why am I the one chasing him down the corridor now?

'How have you done that? How have you turned that on me? You're the one who needs to explain what the fuck is going on. Why am I being treated like some pity party. Why are you saying to Angel that I never get any male attention? You feel sorry for me? The kiss, the shag – was it all a fucking joke?'

'Oh give me strength! If you can honestly stand there and say I did that for a fucking bet or a prank or whatever bullshit you seem to think that was then you're lying to yourself. Whatever that was in there, whatever you've deemed it, it was way fucking more than that to me. How can you not see that? Why must you make this so hard? I'm not your dad. I'm not your stepdad even. I'm not the scum bastard that left you or the arsehole that fucked your mum over. Stop tarring us all with the same brush and finding any excuse to push me away.'

'What's going on with Angel?'

'Nothing.'

I'm tired and I can't keep this crap up. We haven't even begun and there's already drama. I look to the ground, simply to avoid his eyes, and find myself wanting the ground to swallow me whole.

'She's just a young kid who has a thing for me. That's all,' he breathes into my ear. 'I have no feelings for her. Nothing is going on. Nothing will ever go on. I'm friends with her brothers. That's it.'

'Why are you friends with her brothers? With all the shit they get up to? You know there's rumours they deal drugs, don't you? That it isn't actually Daddy's money that pays for all Angel's demands?'

He avoids my gaze upon hearing this, turning away and rubbing the nape of his neck. Does he already know this? Or does he just not want to admit it?

'Look, I've got to go. I've got some work to do. Can we see each other later?' He's almost pleading with me?

'How about the weekend?' I offer in exchange, hoping he gives in easily enough because I don't think I have the willpower to say no again. My body is already burning to get closer to him again, but my head? My head is all over the place. Something doesn't feel right in the pit of my stomach about this whole Angel thing.

If she were out of the picture then I don't think the answer could be clearer – I'd be arranging to meet him back here as soon as my meeting was over, but right now, something just doesn't feel right. I need to talk to Liv – need her to talk some sense into me or make me see what's going on because I just can't see what's seemingly right in front of me.

'I'd prefer to see you sooner if I'm honest, plus I'm out Friday and Saturday night.'

'Well cancel or change your plans then. If you want to see me that badly, you will.'

'Jesus, Jen, you're fucking demanding for saying we're only shagging,' he quips with a half-smile. He clutches my entire jaw in his huge hand and pushes my head back so he only has to lower his slightly to kiss me. 'I'll leave you to get ready and I'll call you later.'

'Am I seeing you at the weekend then or not?' I shout after him as he starts walking to my front door.

'I'll call you later OK?' He looks downtrodden. Defeated. And I have no clue why.

SEVEN

AFTER ANOTHER SHOWER and a quick blow-dry, I'm back looking vaguely presentable for my meeting with the local editor. He's the editor-in-chief at the *Langley Gazette* and heard about me through an old client I wrote for a few years back. I only ever wrote the web content for their spa and their weekly blog, but they gave me total creative licence so I started including some interviews from big names in the industry and I think those gems, the ones that really got my creative juices flowing, are what secured me this interview.

I jump in the car and head to the high street, passing all the usual sights as I do. Tarantino's restaurant, Lavossa the wine bar and of course Hogan's. My favourite bar in the high street. I can enjoy a few cocktails there without being surrounding by what look like fourteen-year-old boys, so Liv and I end up there every time.

The newspaper headquarters are tucked away down a small alleyway that leads to a hidden square where I find the cutest little florist, a pet shop, a small boutique card and gift shop, before I get to the front door of the *Langley Gazette* office.

I love living in Langley. While it isn't smack bang in the middle of London, we're just a twenty-minute train ride into Liverpool Street, which makes it as good as London without the extortionate prices. It also means the news features are often better. Less 'wheelie bin pushed over in torrential downpour' and more 'London crime surge spills over into suburbs' type pieces that you can really sink your teeth into.

I've written a few pieces for the paper, but the contact I've had has only ever been over email. The vast majority of the time, they've emailed asking me for an article that leans toward a particular outcome in support of a product – an editorial paid for by the company perhaps. I get given a host of information and am told to make it within a certain word count. That's it. I've never been called in to meet with the editor before.

I've heard about him though. He's new and he wants to make a name for himself. I heard he doesn't mind rubbing people up the wrong way if it means a good story, and despite my desire to avoid drama in my personal life, I'm all about the drama at work. The bigger the scoop, the more I want to write it.

I push the buzzer and try my best to decipher the crackling voice coming from the other end. 'Umm hi, it's Jen Seaton. I'm here to see the editor, Tristan Trueluck.'

The robotic voice crunches something else down the intercom before the lock buzzes and I can push the door open.

I'm in my dark blue skinny jeans, my heels and my favourite loose-fit blouse. You get a hint of bra underneath it but not enough to make it inappropriate. It's trendy but edgy – the perfect outfit to make a statement at the newspaper. Newspapers are notorious for being filled to the brim with stuffy faces and I want to bring a little spice to the office that reflects my writing style, as well as the utter filth I just took part in in my kitchen, which has been racing through my mind since Eddie left my flat.

I mentally shake myself down and try to put the hot session on the worktop to the back of my mind as I push the final door at the very top of the stairs I've climbed. Bloody hell. I thought riding kept me fit, but this has done me in!

I open the door into a bustling hive of activity. People are moving from one desk to another, papers are flying everywhere and pens are making marks on every surface possible. I bump into a young-looking intern – or at least I assume he's an intern who barely has time to stop – as I shout, 'Tristan Trueluck?'

I just about make out the words 'corner office' and see the vague direction in which he points, and head that way. I come to a huge glass room, separated from the rest of the office, and find a handsome guy sitting at his desk. His gorgeous face peeks up from the screen when I knock. He's got to be in his mid-thirties, younger than I expected. More attractive too. I assumed much older from our phone conversation.

He throws a rather dazzling smile at me and stands up. I begin pushing the door open as he rounds his desk. 'Hi, I'm—'

'Jen Seaton, if I'm not mistaken.'

His smooth voice has me faltering a little. He's absolutely mesmerising in every way. Beautiful to look at and just as handsome when he opens his mouth. There's an air of arrogance about him, but I feel certain he has the expertise to back it up.

I offer my hand and he takes it, holding it for a little longer than I would have expected, causing me to look up from our interlocking handshake to meet his deep blue eyes.

'You aren't mistaken, Mr Trueluck. Pleased to finally put a face to the name.' A very fucking sexy face. My God. One hot shag on the kitchen worktop and I'm salivating over every good-looking man I come into contact with. Calm down, Jen.

'Please, call me Tristan.' He smiles as he gives a gentle squeeze of my hand before letting go. Damn, I was enjoying that.

'Come sit down – make yourself comfortable.' And he ushers me with his hands as he walks to what looks like a drinks fridge. 'Can I get you a drink? Water? Soft drink? Something a little stronger?'

'Water would be great thanks.' I can't help but feel in awe of the guy. He's what, maybe ten years older than me yet he's in a huge corner office running the local paper. Yes, it's not a red top, but come on – it's great here. It's bustling, a real hive of activity, and he's the one calling the shots. I long for the day when I can finally be in that position, though working freelance, that's unlikely to ever happen. I wonder though whether I'd actually be willing to give up the freedom I enjoy so much now for the glamour of a role like this. The pressure alone would be unreal, although by the looks of Tristan, he's under no pressure whatsoever.

'So, Jen, you're no doubt wondering why I called you in. I know we usually keep things pretty distant via email when it comes to getting you to work for us.'

'Yeah, I must admit I did wonder,' I say. Curiosity always gets the better of me – as does my honesty.

'Well, we've been really happy with your work so far and I must admit, I always loved your interview-style blogs over at Sandringham Spa, but I'm wondering if you might be the girl for a particularly hard-hitting piece I have in mind.'

'Absolutely. I've wanted to sink my teeth into something juicy for quite a while now.'

He splutters, and as he does, it sinks in exactly what it is I've just said. I feel myself start to blush, and I can't help but let out a slight giggle. Thank goodness, he does the same and then tries his hardest to get us back onto the straight and narrow in terms of conversation.

'Well, while that's great to know for the office Christmas party, with regards to work, I need to know that you're ready.' And he brandishes that dazzling smile once more.

'Absolutely, Mr True— Tristan. I'm ready for the challenge. Tell me, what's it all about?'

Over the course of the next hour, Tristan proceeds to tell me about the issue our local town appears to have with drug dealing and the people who run the suspected drug ring.

It's not something I'm new to. I have my own suspicions with regards to Angel's brothers, but from what I've been told, this runs incredibly deep. Young kids, around the ages of fourteen, are even being lured into delivering cocaine and weed. Local schools have done their best so far to educate the pupils, as well as the parents, but for the most part, the message appears to be getting lost. What Tristan wants to know is who's at the bottom of it and can I find out more about it. He has a friend within the local police force who's feeding him snippets of information here and there, but he's making little headway, and with a paper to run, he hasn't got time to hit the streets in search of information himself. What he does have, however, is the budget to pay someone like myself to spend time finding out what I can and subsequently creating a blow-up piece. I'll be given a time frame of six months and offered a basic salary along with a card for expenses. I, of course, shake his hand and thank him for the opportunity, promising to get back in touch at the end of the week with a more concrete plan of action.

As I exit the office, I'm nothing short of elated and grab my phone to ring Liv as I walk back to the car. Before I can hit dial, however, a familiar name lights up my screen and makes me smile. 'Hey, Mum,' I sing.

'Hello, darling. I've missed your voice. A text every so often isn't enough, you know. You give that blasted horse more attention than you do me. You certainly buy him more shoes.'

I know she's jesting, but I like to play along with her ridiculous attempts at guilting me into going round for dinner. She still hasn't realised that she doesn't need to play the guilt games, because if there's one thing I love, it's popping back home for some of Mum's grub.

'How about I come round tonight? I can tell you my exciting news.' I mentally block out the kitchen activity with Eddie that suddenly springs into my mind and do my hardest to push my new job offer to the forefront. I can't let this stuff with Eddie, however much I might like him, distract me from this new role. He may have given me the most exciting experience of my life and the most powerful orgasm I've ever had – Christ it was fucking good – but this could be a huge step toward a much bigger career move in the long run. It needs to be my focus.

With a little squeal of excitement, Mum snaps up my offer and tells me to get to hers at 6 p.m. sharp. I tell her I love her and hang up before immediately dialling Liv, but the call goes straight to voicemail.

'Hey, Liv, I have two things to tell you. One, I shagged Eddie in my kitchen today. It was fucking immense but I'm wondering if I should be regretting it massively right now. Things got a little complicated, shall we say, after Angel found out we'd kissed and I got quite the job offer today. I'll explain everything about everything. Just shoot me a text about this weekend, if you're free. What am I talking about? Of course you're bloody free. Hogan's it is. We have a lot to discuss. Heading home to get ready to pop to my mum's so I'll text you a little later.'

I grab the keys for my beat-up hatchback out of my bag. It's small and has more dents in it than I care to admit, but it takes me back and forth to the yard with ease, and if I lower all the seats down, I can fit four bales of beddings and a couple of bags of feed in there, so I love it. Rust and all.

I throw my bag across to the passenger seat, and as I start to put the keys in the ignition, I look around the car park. I'm hardly ever here in the day time. My life revolves around my desk at home and the stables, and that's how I like it. Although I must admit, it's quite refreshing to be here and see what other people get up to day to day. Other people that don't have a great big three-quarter-tonne animal that needs daily attention.

Movement catches my eye as I fire up the engine and I see someone familiar. It's Eddie!

My heart does a little jig in my rib cage, but it comes to an abrupt end as I see him helping a woman out of his car. It's not just any woman either. It's her – Angel.

What the fuck? My heart sinks and my whole body begins to flush, my heart pounding to the point that I can hear it in my ears, and I suddenly feel glued to the spot. I see what can only be described as a stupidly happy smile slapped across her face as she launches herself out of the car and swings her arms around his neck. He looks stiff, not necessarily as happy as I've seen him before, but he's not exactly pushing her off. They're joined by two other men. Those are Angel's brothers. They deal in horses, but as I reminded Eddie earlier, they're trouble – the rumours flying around suggest they deal in more than horses, and it could be that I'm about to find if that's true.

Aside from knowing exactly where I'm heading for information with regards to this new article, I can't help but feel physically sick at the sight of him with her. They look like they're more than friends, and after what we did earlier in the kitchen, I feel betrayed. But should I?

He said that he and Angel are 'complicated' but what the fuck does that mean? Are they shagging too?

I slam my car into gear and screech out of the parking space, heading their way, as the exit lies behind them. I drive past them, toward the exit barrier, and as I do, I see him catch a glimpse of my car and then meet my gaze. Unfortunately for me, he's unable to hide the complete horror in his face, which tells me everything I need to know – Eddie and Angel are more than complicated and I want no part of it.

With water beginning to fill my eyes, I take a harsh right and make my way out of the car park, barely giving the barrier time to lift and let me out. I head for home and fall through my front door in tears, wholly overwhelmed with the situation I've stupidly got myself into and utterly embarrassed at my demonstration of total weakness today.

There's only one thing for it – at the grand old age of twenty-six, I need to see my mum.

EIGHT

I THROW on my riding leggings, looking at the silicone grips on the inside of the knees. They're in the shape of wings and remind me of how much I'd just like to fly away right now. But I'm a grown-arse woman and need to start focusing on what's important and that's not Eddie – or at least it won't be eventually.

I can't help my mind running away with me, thinking of all the reasons he could possibly have for wanting to be with her or even wanting to be with me, but my mind always lands on the same old conclusion: I was merely a shag he'd decided he needed. But the look of horror on his face tells a different story. It tells me he didn't want me to see that. Why wouldn't he want me to see that if he was just looking for a quick fuck?

Grabbing a matching black hoodie, I pick up my riding hat and boot bag, throw them over my shoulder and head out the door. My trainers take me down the stairs with ease, and thanks to their rubber soles, I'm able to make a harsh stop when I get to my security door.

The viewing panel is completely blocked by him.

He's looking at me, with his hand paused over the buzzer. He must have heard me coming down the stairs before he pushed it. What the fuck is he doing here? And without any warning, my mouth follows suit: 'What the fuck are you doing here?'

'I needed to see you.'

'Oh you desperately want to explain why you had Angel draped over your shoulders. Don't worry. I understand. It's complicated,' I shout through the glass though it doesn't stop the sarcasm from penetrating him – I see a definite look of irritation wash across his face. He looks away, biting his tongue and cricks his neck. He instantly looks bigger, more powerful.

'Open. The. Door.'

I press the lock release and push the door into him. He takes a step back and grabs it, pulling it out, but I swerve past him and start getting the car keys out of my bag.

'Just stop for a minute so I can talk to you.'

'Get fucked.'

'Jen, come on!'

'You looked really surprised, Eddie. Didn't want me seeing you with her draped all over you?'

'I was just surprised to see you, that's all. I told you things with Angel are complicated. More than you know, but you need to talk to me. You need to trust me.'

'I had an interview. I got a job, you know. With the *Langley Gazette*. I'll be looking into a few things. The drug problems around here. What's going on, where it's coming from. I'll be looking straight to your mates.'

He freezes. Instantly stops in his tracks and, like a magnet, it pulls me to a halt too. This bothers him more than me seeing him with Angel. What's going on? Something doesn't feel right. Is he involved?

'You shouldn't be getting involved in that. You write content for websites, magazine. You write nice stuff. You don't need to get involved in that sort of stuff. Why? Why would you put yourself in danger like that?'

'Put myself in danger? How? What do you know?'

'Nothing. I just don't think it seems like the right sort of subject for you. People who deal in that sort of stuff are bad news. You go sniffing round that sort of crap and you'll end up getting yourself in a situation where you might get hurt. I don't want that for you.'

'You don't want that for me, or you don't want that for you? Why do I get the impression you know something I don't?'

'Don't be stupid. I'm just looking out for you.' But the look on his face shows worry of a different kind.

'I need to go. I'm riding and then going straight to my mum's.'

'Can you not ride for one evening and just hang out with me,' he says as his hand reaches for my shoulder. He gives it a little squeeze as he moves himself in front of me. 'Jen, I can't stop thinking about you.'

'Sorry, I've got a date with a horse.'

And just like that, I walk away. Something deep in my gut is telling me that this just isn't right. Something is insanely wrong and I can't work out what. Surely he isn't involved in Angel's brothers' dodgy dealings? I know he trims the feet of all the horses they bring in to sell, but I thought it ended there?

I open my car door and look back towards Eddie, still standing where I left him. He looks completely flummoxed. I'm guessing he thought I'd go weak at the knee and invite him back up to scratch another itch for him. Think again. Absolute wanker. This is exactly why I said I wouldn't allow things to go further and he's proved my point for me within a matter of hours.

I lean over to rifle through my bag, which I've just thrown on the passenger seat, and do my usual check of my phone and purse. I've left the flat and made it to the yard way too many times without them so it's become second nature to check.

I sit back up but before I can reach forward and put the key into the ignition, I jump out of my skin and release a blood-curdling scream. The absolute twat is at my window.

'What the fuck! Are you a ninja or something? How did you get to that window so quick? For Christ's sake, you frightened the life out of me!'

He holds my eye contact, my chest now rising fast as I desperately try to catch my breath, but I can't tear my eyes from him. He puts his hand onto the door handle and slowly opens the door. I hear the latch release and even see him adjust his footing. Everything is in slow motion, like he's desperately trying not to scare a small wild animal he's found, which isn't entirely ludicrous considering I look like the proverbial rabbit in the headlights.

He squats down as soon as the door is open wide enough to fit his broad shoulders and gets as close as possible.

'Jen, we've spent years going back and forth with this shit. Haven't we?'

I nod in agreement. He's not wrong. This – whatever *this* is – has been there for years and we've both fought it until now. But it still doesn't make me feel any better about the sick feeling at the pit of my stomach.

'Something's not right. We're not dating, we're not together, I know this, but I still shouldn't see you with another woman draped over you just a couple of hours after we've slept together for the first time.'

'Jen, please. You need to trust me. Just give me a month and she'll be out of my life.'

'Then you need to start being honest with me about what's going on. I'm not blind. This isn't right. I fought this off for the simple fact that I didn't want to be another notch on your bedpost and here I am. That's exactly what I've become.' My perception of what this is doesn't sit well with him – I see him take a deep breath and gather his thoughts.

'Jen, you're far from another notch or a quick shag. I told you that already. Things are complicated for me at the moment and for a number of reasons, one of which being I care about you too much, so I'd rather not get you involved in that side of my life. If you just please give me a month, I promise I'll explain everything when the time is right. You just need to trust me.'

I study him, noting the pain in his eyes. I've never seen him like this. He's always so happy and carefree when he meets me at the yard. There's never a weight so heavy on his shoulders, but right now? Right now he's a different guy entirely.

I don't know if I'm being stupid or not but I give in. 'You're out Friday and Saturday aren't you, so we can meet Sunday. I need some time to think about whatever's going on here.'

'OK, Sunday. I won't lie – I'd rather not wait that long, but if that's all you're giving me, I'll take it.'

He leans in, clutching my knee with one hand and my seat's headrest with the other, then swings in front of me and kisses me with a brute force that lets me know he means it. Then he backs out and shuts the door with a slam and takes a step back.

Trying my best not to look as flustered as I feel, I put the keys in the ignition, check the rear-view mirror and give him a quick wave as I pull off the kerb and head towards the yard.

Within a matter of hours, my life has become even more complicated than I could ever have imagined, and the thought suddenly pops into my head that perhaps Tristan Trueluck knew about my connections with Angel and Eddie before assigning me this project. Could this run much deeper and much closer to home than I previously thought?

I take a quick glance in my rear-view mirror and see Eddie, getting smaller by the second as I drive away from him. My heart physically aches, but I'm not sure if it's because I miss him or because I have a terrible feeling that he's connected to this in a way that will change how I feel about him forever.

NINE

I PULL into the yard and spot Maggy's car, Angel's car and Sarah's car. Sarah and Maggy are pretty good friends of mine. We often do favours for each other to avoid the added cost of services and it works out pretty well.

Maggy gives me a wave as she's walking in from the field with Lincoln and her Shetland and rounds the car. I jump out, ready to take Lincoln off her, and she throws his lead rope over his head as he starts heading toward me. 'Hey, boy,' I whisper as his muzzle comes straight to my face.

I give his body a quick once-over and note the hideous amount of mud all over him. I don't like rugging him up too much. We've had a spell of beautiful weather but had a few light showers overnight which meant him walking out into a pretty muddy field. Thankfully, the sunshine is back out so I can hose all of this crap off and give him a good scrub. This must be one of my favourite things to do with him.

I walk him to the tie-up point and do my usual quick-release knot on the baling twine that's hanging off the metal ring at the wall. 'Safety first,' I tell him as I give his forehead a little tickle.

I leave him standing there and walk into the barn where I'm immediately met with Angel's bitter face. Oh she's pissed off, and at me I presume given the daggers flying at me are on a lethal scale.

'Angel,' I say, like butter wouldn't melt.

'I was going to tie Roman up there.'

'Then fucking tie him elsewhere.' I'm blunt now. All butter has officially melted.

'I saw Eddie this afternoon,' she spits, as if it's all she has left. 'We had a lovely date on the high street.'

'Yes, I saw.'

She looks shocked. She was likely expecting a different reaction. Perhaps a prickly reaction, but I intend on handling this differently.

'I was driving out of the car park and saw him help you out of your car. He didn't look too happy, though I'm not surprised. He'd not long asked to stay at mine for the rest of the day after we fucked on my kitchen worktop.'

I can see Maggy and Sarah peeking out of their stalls, trying to get a better visual of what's actually happening. In all fairness, I have no idea what's happening myself, aside from the fact that I've had enough – it's time to put this little bitch in her place. I really couldn't give a flying fuck who knows what's happening with Eddie and I now; in fact, this could work in my favour. Ruffle a few feathers, Angel might say something she shouldn't with regards to her relationship with Eddie and, more importantly, Eddie's relationship with her brothers.

'My God, we had a mind-blowing time.' OK it's sounding fucking corny now, but I'm past the point of giving a shit. 'And he naturally wanted to stay, but I had to say no. I had an incredible interview with the *Langley Gazette*. They've taken me on for the next six months to investigate the drug problem we seem to be having in this lovely town of ours.'

Well, that's definitely touched a nerve. She looks visibly shaken. But as quickly as the fear appears on her face, it vanishes and is swiftly replaced with anger. Her lip curls, and if she could, I believe she'd be spitting venom right now.

'Let's get one thing straight, sweet cheeks.'

Sweet cheeks? That's a new one.

'You will only ever be a fuck to him. Let's make that very clear. I'm his girlfriend, and I will always be the one for him.'

It hurts, the fact that she's saying that. Her and Eddie are so much more than complicated. Can I seriously be getting caught up in this crap? Do I need to be spending my time fighting with someone who's mentally still a teenager? More to the point, do I really *want* to be fighting over a guy?

I answer my own question with my response. 'It must really hurt that you aren't enough for him. I mean, he looked pretty pissed off to be around you, and from what he's told me, you aren't together. He doesn't really speak with you when you're here together. In fact, the only time you look remotely cuddly is when your brothers are in tow, so I'm guessing it's simply to please them. You aren't actually together, Angel, so I'm curious to know just what you both are? And until I see you both together, I'll continue doing what I want and who I want. And if that happens to include Eddie, on my kitchen worktop, against my stairwell, in the shower or God forbid, in the comfort of my fucking bed, then I will. And if your pathetic little arse still wants to drape yourself over a guy who begged me not to leave him about five minutes ago, deeming you to be nothing more than an irritant he had to put up with for the next month, then so be it.'

I'm aware of just how hypocritical I sound considering that could very well be aimed at me as much as it is her. Do I want to be draped all over a man who's spent time with her today? No, not at all, but I won't let this rude, indignant little cow know that.

I leave her open-mouthed at my far-from-expected and rather spiteful response and head to my stall to grab my grooming tools. By the time I've turned around, Roman has been put in his stall and Angel is in her car, reversing up the forecourt and heading out of the yard. I guess I won that ridiculously childish battle.

I throw my grooming tools down at Lincoln's feet, making him spook, and physically sag as I realise how I just reduced myself in there. In front of Maggy and Sarah too.

Sarah emerges out of the barn, trying to avoid eye contact, and ties up her sweet Friesian cross mare before she ventures over. 'Don't hate yourself too much. She's needed a good dressing-down for years. She's lacked the parents that should have done it a long time ago. You needed to stand your ground and you did a great job.'

'I feel pathetic.'

'Why? You had a great shag with a bloke we all know is single. Let's face it. They aren't in a relationship. Whatever the fuck is going on there is more to do with her brothers than her. She's just taking advantage of that and trying desperately to put you in your place like she does everybody else. You've done nothing wrong, girly. Even if you shagged him every fucking week. So what? You're two consenting adults. That's all that needs to be said.'

'I asked him about Angel and he just said that it's complicated.' I perch myself on the edge of the mounting block, twirling my dandy brush around in my hand. 'You know the rumours flying around about her brothers, don't you?'

Sarah looks up from her grooming kit. 'Well yeah, everybody does. I don't think they're rumours either. Nor are the ones about Angel.'

'What rumours about Angel?'

'That they bloody well pimp her out! How have you not heard that? Jimmy's heard through the grapevine on more than one occasion.' Sarah's husband works in a mechanics just off the high street. He also happens to have some amazing CCTV cameras all around there. Not that he'd ever watch the footage. He only has them up to help reduce his insurance premiums, so Sarah told me. I wonder if he'd let me watch the cameras to see if anything untoward goes on around there when the sun goes down?

My index finger trails a circle on my chin as I wonder about my next move for this article, but I'm soon knocked out of my trance as Lincoln starts pawing the ground. 'Ooh haynet. Sorry, boy.'

I run into the barn, grab a haynet and start giving him a good brush, getting the insane amount of dried on mud off of his coat so Sarah and I can go for a quick whiz around the hay field before I head to my mum's for dinner.

Maggy very kindly brings us a cuppa each and props herself against the mounting block so we can all natter while we groom and drink a good old stables cup of tea. That means dirty chipped mugs and most likely a few strands of hay floating around in the cup.

We throw on our tack, grab our helmets and our boots and mount, waving goodbye to Maggy as she heads into the school to start her groundwork with her Shetland pony.

The hack around the hay field is everything I need it to

be. It's peaceful, uncomplicated and generally lovely. The two horses are absolutely fab. Zara, Sarah's mare, is as chilled out as she usually is despite Lincoln continually trying to get her attention by nibbling her neck, and we chat about anything and everything. Sarah tells me all about her latest project at the mechanics. She does the marketing for the company, which she's now franchised, and it sounds like it's starting to take off, which is awesome. I'm so pleased for her and Jimmy because they've worked their backsides off getting the mechanics off the ground, taking it further than either of them imagined.

Later, when Lincoln is back at his tie-up point and I'm hosing him down, my phone flashes. It's him.

EDDIE: What happened with Angel?

JEN: Why?

EDDIE: I don't need you getting involved. Please just trust me when I say in a month all of this will be over with.

JEN: She verbally abused me. She deserved what she got.

EDDIE: I really don't need you riling her up right now.

JEN: Once you tell me what the fuck is going on, maybe I'll take a back seat. Until then, things are going to get 'riled up' if she continues with the bullshit in public.

I STARE AT MY PHONE, wondering what the hell he's got himself into and make a mental note to speak with Liv tomorrow about it all. She's all too familiar with Angel's brothers – one of them at least; they dated for about six months. He was as vague and as secretive as she'd expected, but she was also doing her best to get over her first love at the time so she did it the only way she knew how – by getting under someone else. In her defence, it worked. Apparently he was an animal in the sack, and that's exactly what she needed – a good shag to take her mind off her broken heart. Then when she stopped getting excited to see him, she cut it off. I don't think Damion was too pleased about it, but being who he was, he did his utmost not to show it and simply brandished her a 'tart I've been shagging for a bit' to anyone that would listen.

With Liv, it was water off a duck's back. She didn't care one iota and that was that. I wish I had her resilience.

The sun is shining and the weather is glorious. I finish hosing Lincoln off, give him a good scrub with my dandy brush and some tea tree shampoo – which, I might add, costs more than my own brand anti-dandruff shite – and pop him in his freshly laid stall. He dives straight into his feed and I do my three-point check over the door before I walk away – water, feed and hay. I'm good to go.

I wave goodbye to Maggy and Sarah, reminding her that I'll pop Lincoln and her Shetland Scrappy out in the morning together before I jump in my car and head to Mum's. The hack was exactly what I needed. The confrontation with Angel absolutely was not.

TEN

I ARRIVE at my mum's just before 6 p.m. and grab my bag from the passenger seat, hauling it over the handbrake and jumping out onto the kerb. I look down at my shit attempt at parking. Taxi to the kerb, Jen.

I throw open my mum's front gate and march up the pathway before giving the knocker a good thwack. As always she's there in an instant.

'Peach. I've missed you. I can't believe you've actually taken time out of your schedule to come and visit your mother. Come here.' And she throws her arms around me as she always does, whether I've been away five weeks or five minutes. I love my mum. She's just what I need after what can only be described as a truly confusing bloody day.

I love my mum's house. It's narrow, a galley-style home, but it's so cosy and always so warm and welcoming. We used to live in a huge house as a kid, but my stepdad paid for it, so when he left Mum for a younger model, the house went with him. Mum got shafted completely, despite paying half the bills, and we wound up homeless. But she got up, dusted herself down and got out there and worked her socks off until she could afford to buy a place that was ours. After my stepdad cheated on her, getting some young bit of stuff – as my mum used to call her – pregnant, Mum vowed never to go near another man again. And true to her word, she never has.

I walk into the hallway and hang my coat on my usual hook after she's put me down. She never complains that I probably stink of horse either. It's just one of the things I love about my mum. She's not an animal person in the slightest, but she never moans and always, always asks about my man.

And as if on cue: 'How is the brute?'

'Oh he's dreamy as ever. You know.' And I give her the cheesy dazzled smile I always do when I declare how much I love my horse.

'Did you have a good ride, Peach?' She's called me Peach ever since I can remember. I've always loved it too.

'You could say that,' I mumble as we move into the kitchen and I lower myself into a chair at the dining table.

'Oh?' She looks at me, waiting for the next bit of the story, kettle hovering above the cups.

I've always been completely honest with my mum, always telling her exactly what's going on with my love life. My mum insisted on an open relationship as soon as my stepdad did the dirty. She didn't want me hiding things from her, and yet in spite of the way she'd previously been treated, she always insisted I had a better attitude toward men than she did. She never wanted to 'taint' me was how she used to put it.

She's always loved Eddie too and, like Liv, has always given me a little nudge in his direction. As with most things in my life, she can see it plain as day, but I unfortunately never can. The problem is that when I tell her what's happened, I'm not sure she's going to feel the same way.

'I slept with Eddie, Mum.' I look at her from under my eyelashes, still ever so slightly ashamed to be admitting to having sex in front of her. I don't think that feeling ever goes away, does it?

Her look of excitement is killing me, but it soon drops when she doesn't see that I'm exactly happy about it.

'Was it that terrible?'

Oh God, Mother!

'For Christ's sake, Mum!'

'What? I only ask because you look so bloody miserable about it? What's wrong? Has he humped and dumped you?'

'Jesus Christ, Mum. Where on earth did you hear that? He hasn't humped and dumped me... as such. I believe I may have humped and dumped him though.'

'Ooh a little female empowerment, eh? Nothing wrong with a little scratch of the old itch.'

So that's where I get that saying from.

'But you know, one look at him tells me he can't be bad in bed so I have to wonder why you've run for the hills? Not all men are like your father – or your stepfather for that matter.'

'Mum. Stop. It's nothing to do with them. Things are just... complicated,' I say, taking Eddie's words and using them as if they were my own.

She's now going to ask me, 'How exactly are they complicated?' which she does and I stumble on my answer. 'Well? Spit it out?'

'There's another woman, kind of.'

'OK, I'm going to need a little more detail here, Peach.'

'There's another woman down the yard – Angel.'

'Oh not that little crank?'

'Yes, that little crank,' I confirm as she fills the mugs with water, adds a splash of milk and squeezes the teabags before tossing them in the bin.

'Come on, this isn't dining-table discussion. This is feet up-on-the-sofa-with-a-pack-of-biccies discussion.' And she grabs a packet of malted milks before heading into the living room.

I walk in to find she's got a blanket on the arm of the sofa for me, popped my tea on the little table next the sofa and put the footstool in front of where she wants me to sit. She then heads to her favourite armchair and curls up.

'The dinner's in the crockpot and won't be ready for a bit yet so spill the beans. This needs to get sorted before it gets you any more upset than it already has. Are they together?'

'Angel and Eddie? No. There was always rumours about them, and whenever we've bumped into each other at Hogan's, she's always appeared. Made a beeline for him. And now she's found out something happened so wham, there she is.'

'What do you mean wham there she is?'

'She's latched on to him, digging her claws in further and telling me they're together and I'm just a pity screw.'

'And what does Eddie say about it?'

'He says it's complicated. But I can't help but think it's not complicated because he's actually with her, but because something's going on with her older brothers.'

'You mean Damion and Alfie?'

'Yeah.'

'Hmmm, that's not good, you know. I knew their mother. She struggled with them when they were younger, and when she passed, they ran riot. The father was never interested unless he could make a penny from them. I didn't see much involvement from him to be honest.'

'Yeah well, I'm seeing plenty of involvement from Angel right now and she needs to fuck off.'

'I honestly don't know what to suggest, my love. What's your gut feeling?'

'That something isn't right but it's not the obvious.'

'And the obvious is?'

'Cheating. I don't think he's actively cheating on me – I mean we've only slept together and kissed once. It's not like we're dating.'

'No, I know you young kids discuss exclusivity and all that crap now, but you at least want respect from a man, knowing he isn't dipping his wick elsewhere.'

I blush at her last comment. Mum can be pretty candid at times and I don't know any of my friends that can have these sorts of conversations so openly with a parent. I pick up my mug and wrap both hands around it, enjoying the warmth that fills them. Hopefully it can warm up the cold feelings I currently have toward Eddie.

Mum must notice my sudden slip into deep thought, as she gives me a little verbal nudge. 'Anyway, enough about men. Tell me about this exciting news.' And she wiggles her hips and wraps a stupid grin across her entire face, hissing when a little tea slips from her mug onto her hands.

I burst out laughing, and just like that, Mum's made me feel better. As she always does.

I tell her about the job offer, including the rather handsome editor Tristan, but it doesn't take her long to see the link between what I need to start delving into for the story and the current mishmash that is my love life.

'So you think the Drafter brothers are drug dealers? That's not exactly far-fetched. But you think Eddie is involved in that part too? He's their farrier, sweetheart. What do you think he does? Drug runs between stable yards?'

My face suddenly drops and look at her with surprise. 'What if he does, Mum?'

'Oh don't. A Casanova Eddie may be, but a drug runner? No, sorry. I may have little faith in men, but I just can't see young Eddie running drugs for the Drafter brothers.'

'No, maybe not.'

'But my God, sweetie, my Peach! I honestly couldn't be more proud of you right now. Getting such a job, such a big story and all through word of mouth. Baby, you are one heck of a writer. This editor sounds a bit of a dish too.' And she wiggles her hips again, only this time she focuses on her cup of tea a little more, careful not to singe her hands again.

'Come on, love; I think dinner's ready. Let's go eat.'

No verbal invite's actually needed though – I can already smell her amazing casserole. God, I love mum's cooking.

We have a lovely evening, watching reality shite on the TV, moaning about the fact that it's shite but refusing to turn it over. We then spend more time watching people watching TV, which I still don't quite understand but still somehow enjoy. Especially the celebrity version.

Just as it's getting dark, I steal a kiss, give her a hug and make a move.

Despite the night with Mum being exactly what I needed it to be, I still can't quite shift the feeling that something isn't right with Eddie. He's involved in something that he shouldn't be, or am I just desperately looking for an explanation that doesn't involve him shagging Angel and royally taking the piss out of me?

Mum, bless her, was worried, I could tell but I've made a promise to keep her in the loop and keep my head held high at all times.

I will not lower myself to shitty standards or get involved in some hideous love triangle. I'm better than that, and by God, I *deserve* better.

ELEVEN

I WAKE up feeling so tired but my alarm gives me no other option but to shift my arse out of bed. I left my phone on charge on the other side of my room when I couldn't get to sleep last night so I'd be forced to get up. Thankfully, my plan worked and I'm up and dressed by 5 a.m.

I have a quick protein shake, brush my teeth and I'm jumping in my car by 5.30 a.m. The roads are empty and it's dark still. A fox scurries across the road and I see a few rabbits' eyes light up as I drive through the country lanes on the way to the yard.

I pull in but see a small light on in the barn. The main light isn't switched on just yet so I turn my headlights off and stop just shy of the barn in an attempt not to blind everyone or wake up the rest of the sleeping ponies with my larger-than-life engine.

I walk quietly to the main entrance of the barn, where I usually tie Lincoln up, but I'm brought to an abrupt halt when I hear voices. That's when I actually take notice of the car and the van parked outside. It's Angel and Eddie.

I feel physically sick. Have I just walked in on some

secret rendezvous? He's probably whispering sweet noth-ings into her ear, telling her I mean nothing. I want to turn and run instead of facing whatever's going on in there, but I can't bring myself to leave. My feet won't turn – the only way they move is forward. And the voices suddenly become less muffled. I'm not sure I want to hear this.

'I swear to God, if you keep seeing her, I'll tell my brothers you're upsetting me.'

'Oh fuck off, Angel. Your brothers couldn't give a flying fuck about your scrawny little arse. The only reason they keep you around is to make money off you when they pimp you out to any scrote that'll pay for it.'

'That's not true. I'm in control of my life!' She's screaming at him now.

'No, you're not. How do you not see that? You're not in control. You. Are. Being. Sold. For. Sex. By. Your. Brothers!'

I gasp but stifle the noise with my hoodie sleeve.

'I told you I wouldn't leave you alone with them. I told you I would get you and I away from this shit. I promised your mum before she died. And I'll keep that promise when the time is right, but right now you need to back the fuck off of Jen.'

'What do you see in that uptight little bitch?'

'Watch your fucking mouth, Ang. I won't have one more word said about her. You stop telling her we're together. We're *never* going to be together. We never were, and we never will be. You need to realise that just because I'm seeing Jen, doesn't mean I'm leaving you with them. I'm just as entwined in this bullshit as you are. I promised I would get us both out of it and I mean it. Just give me time.'

'How? How the fuck are you going to get us out of it. You know better than I do that they own our arses.'

I hear footsteps moving further away from me and then everything goes quiet.

I hover outside the barn for another five minutes before I can bring myself to move. I can't hear another word and haven't been able to for a while.

I can't leave – Lincoln is in there. I need to turn him out with Scrappy. I take a deep breath and pluck up the courage to walk in. As I turn into the barn through the huge sliding doors, I'm met with two uncomfortable-looking faces.

Angel is the first to say something. 'Oh fuck off. You. It's always you.' And she takes an immediate about-turn, slamming her empty stall door shut, then walking out to her car. Both Eddie and I watch in silence as she pulls out of the yard.

I turn to face him and see a glimmer of the Eddie I know, but he looks tired, like he has the weight of the world on his shoulders. I instantly feel the need to wrap my arms around his shoulders after hearing him tear into Angel, but I'm still cautious that I'm not comfortable with this entire situation.

'Jen, I don't want you to do this story.'

'That's what you want to talk about right now? My work?'

'Jen, listen to me. I need you to turn this story down. For me. Please. You have no idea what you're getting yourself into.'

'And what exactly do you know about it?'

'I know enough. You need to trust me – please, Jen.'

'What do you not want me to find out? What were you talking about with Angel?'

'How long were you there for? You shouldn't be listening to my private conversations, Jen. All you need to do is trust me!'

He takes a step toward me, but I can see he's nervous now he knows I overheard things I shouldn't have. He rakes a hand through his thick dark curls and takes it down to the nape of his neck.

I can't help but step toward him and rub his shoulder, slowly moving my hand up toward his neck. It's like a natural instinct to do whatever I can to make him feel better. I have no idea where it comes from considering I spent most of this morning deciding exactly to what degree I hate him.

As soon as I touch him, he turns into me, closing the gap and wrapping me in his arms. The embrace is something my body naturally responds to. I belong here. I don't want to ever leave, but I need to get to the bottom of this... weird relationship, whatever it is, with Angel.

I give myself an extra few inches on my tiptoes and feel him sigh into my neck.

'You need to trust me with whatever's going on here, Ed. You keep saying you want... whatever this is between us, but I can't do this if you don't trust me with whatever it is you're dealing with. What are you caught up in?'

'I can't, Jen. I just can't,' he murmurs as he sags further into me.

'Then neither can I.'

I pull his arms from around my waist and step out of his embrace. My body cries out for his touch; it feels empty without him, and my heart is screaming at me to kiss him – to run my hands through his hair, but my head is leading on this one and it's stopping me from getting hurt.

He takes my hand in his, rubbing his thumb across the top and over my wrist. My body responds immediately with that familiar throb between my legs as he turns my hand over and trails his forefinger along the inside of my wrist and down my palm.

He steps toward me and curls his arm around my neck. I see his eyes. They've glassed over and he looks choked up.

My free hand moves up to his face as he lowers his head to kiss me on the cheek. I feel him take a deep breath at the side of my face as he kisses me again before he drops my hand and starts walking out of the barn.

That's it. We're done before we even started.

I take a step back and find myself sitting on the grooming box outside someone else's stable. Lincoln calls to me as I hear the sound of Eddie's van turning over, and instinctively I go to the only man who's never broken my heart. I walk into his stall and cry into his shoulder. He just stands there sniffing me, just letting me rest before he nudges my side and nickers for me to look at him.

In total silence, I put his rain sheet on, buckling it up at the chest before crossing over the surcingles underneath. All the while, Lincoln keeps an eye on me, looking up from his feed every so often to check I'm OK. I pick out his feet and then walk out, making my way to Scrappy. In true 'Shitland' style, he couldn't care less how I'm currently feeling and still tries to bite my arse as I pull his mini rain sheet on too. I pick out his feet too then pop his headcollar and lead rope on, dodging his teeth the whole time.

I'm in a daze and can't stop thinking about what's just happened. I feel sick to the pit of my stomach knowing the rumours about Angel are true. No wonder she is how she is. Her own brothers are selling her for sex, and I've taken the interest of what appears to be the only man she can trust. No wonder she hates me, and in all fairness, if I were in her shoes... I'd probably hate me too. My main concern right now, however, is how exactly Eddie is wrapped up in this shitshow?

And then it dawns on me. This is what my job entails. If I do it properly and expose the people behind the drug problems we've been having, I'm going to expose Angel and Eddie too. Fuck. I was right –Tristan must know about my connection to them. He has to.

I pull my phone from my pocket and write a quick email to Tristan.

JEN: Did you know my connection to the Drafter brothers when you assigned me to this story?

I BARELY MAKE it to the field before my phone dings and I see I've received a reply from Tristan.

TRISTAN: Let's meet for lunch. Today – 12 p.m. at Lavossa's.

JEN: See you there. Bring the company card. It's on you.

TRISTAN: Naturally, gorgeous.

GORGEOUS? Cheeky fuck actually thinks he's going to get away with charming his way out of this one.

I thrust the phone back in my pocket and turn both horses out in the field. I can't believe this. I can't believe I've been so bloody naive. I also can't believe how quickly I'm jumping to conclusions lately, although in all fairness, I was pretty right about Eddie. He is involved in this somehow, though at least he's not cheating on me. OK, and breathe, Jen. Just breathe.

I stand at the gate and watch Lincoln and Scrappy walk over the brow of the hill in their paddock and see Roman charge toward them. Just like his owner, he's loud, in your face and irritating at times. But Lincoln, unlike his owner, seems to shrug it off easily. Maybe I should be more like Lincoln? A little more understanding of what's actually going on right now. She doesn't know I know the full details, but I certainly understand her a lot more now.

Once I've mucked Lincoln's stall out, prepped it for this evening and swept along the barn, I close his door and head to the car. The key goes into ignition and Bonnie Tyler's 'It's A Heartache' comes blaring on the radio.

'Fucking isn't it just,' I mutter to myself as I make my way home in the now pouring rain. Could this day get any worse?

Stupid question. Very stupid question.

TWELVE

I MADE a mad dash from the car to the front security door of my flat but still end up absolutely soaked. I drag my backside up the communal stairs and let myself into my empty flat. It suddenly feels a whole lot emptier after how I left things with Eddie. I can't help but feel not only heartbroken but enraged by the shite that is my life and what I seem to have become involved in – or not involved in now, as the case may be.

I jump in the shower, shave my legs, scrub everywhere and give my hair a real good seeing to. I think I'm subconsciously trying my best to scrub this morning off me. But however much I try, that hideous sinking feeling just won't leave me.

I sit myself at my desk for most of the morning, totally absorbed by my architectural client's brief. I draft three of the new pieces they've commissioned and send them over for approval before taking a peek at my phone. It's 11.30 a.m. I've got thirty minutes to get ready and get myself to Lavossa, which shouldn't take too long. It's ten minutes, if that, in the car. I notice I've got another text from Liv too. Shit.

I was supposed to reply to her last night. That'll earn me an ear-bashing. I quickly text her back.

JEN: Tomorrow night at Hogan's if you fancy. Lots to tell. Be there... please.

ALMOST INSTANTLY MY phone lights up in reply.

LIV: Fucking obviously with the week you've had, love. I need you to dish! xx

JEN: Promise I will. See you tomorrow at about 7 p.m. Usual spot if some twat hasn't pinched our table ;-)

I CHUCK my phone in my bag and check myself in the mirror, taking in the lion's mane of frizz that is my hair. I can't go out like this. I whizz my cheap and cheerful straighteners over it, taming it enough to make me presentable, then throw on some cute tapered trousers that sit at the ankle, my black stilettos and a white tank top. I put my red blazer on top and throw on a long Tiffany chain to finish it off. Then I remind myself that I'm doing this simply to look professional, not attractive for Tristan. I know it's not uncommon to get work through your connections, and maybe I should just be grateful that I've got my foot in the door – and with such a massive story too – but that doesn't change the fact that he's an arsehole, and I'm done with other people's bullshit today.

THIRTEEN

I ARRIVE at Lavossa's looking half decent, though feeling maybe a smidgen less than that. Recent activities have definitely taken their toll, so I give myself a mental telling off and do my best to buck my ideas up. Stand tall, hold your head high and do not let the side down, girly.

I spot Tristan amongst a sea of locals, all diving into their meals and enjoying a glass of wine or two, and feel my mouth already watering at the thought of a glass of white tomorrow night with Liv.

Tristan spots me and stands. As he lifts his hand, I start making my way over to him. My cheeks begin to flush the closer I get to him and he notices. Of course he notices.

'Did you run here, Jen? You look a little flushed?' His full-on grin is bashed away in a hideous attempt to look half serious, but he can't hide his lips curling at the edges. He wants to laugh and I want to put my hands around his neck. I ignore him.

He pulls my chair out for me and lightly brushes the small of my back as I pass him, guiding me to my chair. I don't hate the feeling of him touching me. But I hate that I don't hate it.

'Well, I can't say it was an unpleasant surprise to receive your email this morning. It gives me immense pleasure seeing your name pop up on my phone like that.'

I fake a smile and a nod, indulging him for a few seconds before I pounce. 'Let's cut the crap, Tristan.'

He looks taken aback at my abruptness, but I'm out of patience now.

'Why did you hire me? Because you thought I'd be right for the story or because you knew about my connection to the Drafter brothers?'

'What does it matter? You're a great writer either way. I wouldn't hire someone who couldn't write for shit, would I? My name's on the line as much as yours, gorgeous.'

'Don't call me gorgeous.'

'I'd rather call you that than babe or honey – so bloody Essex. Besides, you are gorgeous. Are you not?'

'Let's just keep things professional, shall we?'

He raises his eyebrows and shifts in his seat before leaning back against his chair, looking more casual and, might I add, fuckable than ever. This isn't going to go as planned.

'Why did you hire me?' I ask again.

'Oh for Christ's sake, gorgeous— sorry, Jen.' He throws his hands in the air in a pathetic attempt to look sorry. 'Yes, fine, I hired you because of your connection to the Drafter brothers. I've seen you talking with them. However, may I just put it out there that I did know of you before I found out that you were loosely connected?'

'If you know about Damion and Alfie, what they're up to, why not go after them yourself? Do the digging yourself?'

'Oh come on, it's a bit bloody obvious, isn't it? Do you not think they have a rough idea of who I am?'

'You're not exactly famous, Tristan. You're the editor of a local paper. Calm yourself down.'

'Thank you, my sweet girl. I'm more than aware of that, but the likes of Damion and Alfie have connections in high places and know better than to talk to a story-hungry journo like me.'

I have to admit he's right. But if everything is so glaringly obvious, which it is, why has he not gone to the police?

'What about the police? Why not just go to them?'

'Oh come on, don't make me regret hiring you, my darling. As I said before, they have friends in high places and those friends include a few local law-enforcement officers who are on payroll, namely to ensure they look away when needed.'

'Even when it comes to pimping out young girls?'

'Even when it comes to pimping out young girls, Jen, yes.' His head lowers and he combs his fingers through his hair, sweeping it off of his face. He leans back as he does so and his expression is almost concerned. Is he genuinely interested in this story for the sake of the people involved?

'So what do you know about me and my connections?'

'Well, that's a much more enlightening story, isn't it? I know you have a horse stabled at the same yard or centre.' He purposely elongates the word centre to emphasise the fact that he hasn't a fucking clue what he's talking about. 'As has that Angel girl. I also know you're close with that farrier guy...'

He looks me dead in the eye and I get the impression he's trying to see if I'm more than just close. Is he trying to work out if I'm more involved with him than his first impression had led him to think?

'What do you know about Eddie? He shoes all the Drafters' horses.'

'I know he's involved. And I know he's caught your eye. Are you together?'

I think for a moment and wonder if we are or we aren't, but given the way we left things this morning, it can only be a resounding no.

'You'd be wise to steer clear of him, gorgeous. I'm sure we could find someone much better suited to a woman of your talents.'

That dazzling smile lights up his face again and I can't help but smile in return.

'Professional, remember?'

'Yes, sorry, but you know I'm right. Are you two involved? I'm asking for the story, that's all. It's valuable information.'

I know he's lying about his reasons for asking, but he's not wrong. It is relevant.

'We were involved briefly. And by briefly, I mean a one-time thing.'

'You dark horse, you. I never put you for a one-night stand type of girl.' And he mockingly shoves my arm. 'But believe me, you're better off without him. He's involved in this more than you realise – more than I think too. I just need to find out how much.'

'I know I sound biased here but I really don't think he'd willingly be involved in drugs or selling young women for sex. It's just not him. I've known Eddie for years and I just can't see it.'

'Then open your eyes, sweetheart. The more digging you do into this, the more you're going to find out, and believe me, you won't like what you see. So are you still in?'

I hate the thought that Eddie could be tangled up in this

mess. Equally, I hate the thought of giving up on this story simply to save my relationship with a potential drug dealer.

'Yes, I'm in.'

I stare at the glass of water that's just been placed on the table, then give the waiter a quick glance and a courteous smile, but I feel anything but grateful right now. This isn't where I pictured myself just a few weeks ago. Not at all.

'Well that's good news. I thought I was going to have get on my knees and beg. I'm not averse to it, you know... just for the record.' He glances up from his drink as he takes a gulp, watching me over the rim of the glass as the penny drops.

'You're pretty forward for someone in a high-powered position at a newspaper. Some would say this verges on sexual harassment, you know.' I gently finger my glass, making shapes in the condensation on the outside of the glass. I'm not being threatening. I'm not warning him. I'm bloody well flirting! What the fuck am I doing?

He chuckles and raises his hands, mocking me with an over-the-top sarcastic face.

'A guy can't tell a girl he likes her anymore?'

My eyes dart up to meet his to find he's now looking anything but funny. His expression is suddenly very serious and he's gauging my reaction.

As an employer, he's overstepped the mark. But in all honesty, I'm not recoiling at what he's just said. I'm not sure if it's the hot fucking mess that is my current emotional state or the simple fact that he's an absolute god to look at, but my body reacts in a way that gives him his answer without me saying a word. I blush and cross my legs, desperate not to let him see me squirm or the small smile that creeps across my face.

Tristan Trueluck is a good-looking man. He's a very good-looking man with an air of power about him that makes him all the more sexy, but is he any better for me right now than Eddie, a guy who, let's face it, has had my heart for years?

'What's say we finish up here after a quick bite and head back to the office to go over the information I've already got and where we need to go from here?'

'We? You're working on the piece as well?' I can't help the small glimmer of excitement that shows in my voice as I find out that Tristan and I are going to be spending a lot of time together over the coming six months. I can't deny that I was excited about sinking my teeth into this project with just me at the sail, but the thought of working under someone with so much experience just seems like too good an opportunity to miss.

I just wonder if it's a little dangerous working so closely with Tristan considering his obvious fondness for me and his inability to hide it in any professional manner. There's no way I'm the first woman he's spoken to like this, and I doubt I'll be the last, but Tristan has a certain warmth to him. A warmth that makes it difficult to dislike him.

'I am indeed, gorgeous.'

'Why are you so hot on this one? It's not like it's anything new.'

'Let's say there's a personal tinge to this one. But you already knew that, didn't you, Jen?'

There's definitely an air of arrogance about him, but it's earned. Earned in a way that makes it less arrogance and more confidence. He's self-assured because he got to where he is through sheer grit and determination. I read up on the guy after our first meeting. He had nothing handed to him.

Nothing. His parents divorced at a young age, and he was brought up in foster care after his mother spiralled out of control following a struggle with drugs. I would be foolish to think this story is anything but a personal mission for him, and I never needed him to tell me, but I'd prefer he had than admit I've done my research.

'I may have read up on you a little...'

'Ooh, I feel famous.' His cocky grin has dropped, replaced by a look of annoyance. Not at me, I don't think. But at his past perhaps?

What happened to his mum was years ago. Years before the likes of the Drafter brothers could have even rolled their first joint, let alone started dealing, so while this isn't directly related to his mother, I get the link. I just wonder if it's all a little too close to home.

'Sorry. I didn't mean to dig too deep. I just need to know what I'm dealing with, who I'm dealing with. You'd do the same I'm sure.'

'Absolutely. Besides, I'm not annoyed. It's just something I'd rather not think about right now, especially when I'm having lunch with a beautiful woman.' And the cocky grin is back.

This will undoubtedly be a challenging job, not simply because we're digging into what could potentially be a very dangerous aspect of our local town, but because it would appear I have a crush on my boss, who I'll also be working very closely with. Suddenly Eddie walking out on me is the least of my worries. While my heart may be crushed by his exit from the barn this morning, at least I can't get into any more trouble with him. Tristan, on the other hand, looks like he could be a whole lot of trouble for me if I don't stick to my guns and keep things as professional as I can.

He keeps his eyes on me, as if he's trying to read what I'm thinking, but I pick up the menu and avoid his eye contact as best I can. He doesn't miss the grin that slowly creeps across my face though. Oh God, this is going to be hard.

FOURTEEN

AFTER LUNCH, we make our way back to the office and go over all the information he has already. It's awesome to see him instantly change as he walks into his office. The cocky smile is still there but that's just him; otherwise his whole persona changes. He almost has a serious air about him. It's a total transformation and I'm in awe as he discusses the case, showing me the evidence he'd already got. He'd hired private investigators before but they stopped working for him after one of them was roughed up and spread the word within the industry. Hence why he came in search of me. He knows about Angel. He also happens to know more than one of the local police force has been in contact with her – and it wasn't to offer help.

From what he's telling me, the Drafter brothers have a tendency to get their targets nice and drunk before setting their sister to them and taking photographic evidence. The officers end up petrified and subsequently in their pockets through fear of the incriminating photographs being brought to light.

I feel sick at seeing what Angel is capable of, but I'm

starting to realise more and more how this is anything but voluntary on her part. She looks more than comfortable in these photographs, but her conversation this morning with Eddie proves otherwise.

Again, my instant thought is why they simply can't go to the police, to someone who isn't involved, but I'm informed pretty quickly by Tristan that it simply isn't possible.

'Damion, Alfie – these guys are just the tip of the iceberg, gorgeous. They work for some very unscrupulous men that could do some very awful, awful things to anyone that gets in their way. It goes way beyond this town, sweetheart. We just happen to be the unlucky bastards because we have a port so close by where their drugs come in.'

'Fine. So we can't go to the police, but if they're as dangerous as you say they are, what the fuck are you going to do with any evidence that we manage to get? Print the story and run? Because from what I see, we'd be just as stupid to get ourselves involved in this.'

'I get what you're saying, I do, but it's down to us to make this public. It's down to us to get the story out there. If we can get enough hard evidence, we can take it higher up, to someone who does have the bollocks to actually deal with it. I have a few friends in the force who said I need more than what I have. I need to build up a case that will put them behind bars.'

'Why aren't the police looking at it themselves? I mean outside of this area? Higher up or whatever it is you're alluding to here?'

'They are – we're just one of a few different pieces within this puzzle who need to do their bit in order to bring it all together.'

'What do you know about Eddie? How is he involved in all of this?'

'I know they've got him running drugs from multiple locations. The guy travels the length and breadth of the county. Doesn't take much for him to pick up from them and take it wherever they need it to go. I've even seen him run in the city on more than one occasion. He drops off the package and leaves. Granted, he never looks happy about it, but he does it all the same.'

'Do you think they have something on him?'

'Quite possibly. That's how they get all their minions working for them.'

I wince at the description of Eddie, the big strong alpha male I know him to be, as a minion. It's starting to get to me, knowing just how involved he is in all of this, and I need a break. I rise from my chair and stare at the pictures in front of me. Scattered everywhere I see Angel's face, her brothers, as well as other faces; some I recognise as business owners in this town, some I don't. What I don't see is Eddie. This tells me one of two things: either he isn't as involved in the actual drug deals or the selling of the drugs to the local kids around here, or he's simply better at keeping out of sight. What I do know is that I need to find out what's going on, and I need to find out now.

'You leaving, gorgeous?' Tristan looks up at my body towering over his and I'm sure I see a slight movement in his hand. It's as if he almost considers touching the leg I have closest to him.

'Yeah, I need to sit down and think about all of this. Take it all in. Digest it, you know?'

'Yeah sure. Fancy a drink?'

I look at him, shocked he wants to let this spill past the office once more and raise my eyebrow at him. 'No, no drink. I'm going home.'

'Suit yourself.' He shrugs and stands up next to me. His

tall frame suddenly seems much broader now the suit jack-et's gone. He's relaxed in the few hours we've been here going over the work he's already done. He's been proud. Happy almost, like he's showing off his treasures. I know he's got a secret kick out of the fact that he's shown me Eddie is more involved in this than I first thought.

His top two buttons are undone and his sleeves are rolled up. He looks calm and at home now he's in his own domain. I, on the other hand, feel dejected and sick.

I start pulling my blazer back on and slide my phone into my back pocket, but as my hand swings round, padding my front pocket for my purse, he reaches out and gently takes my fingertips in his hand, careful not to push it too far and touch my actual body. 'You sure I can't convince you to come for that drink with me?'

I can't deny the feeling of him touching me is nothing short of exciting. I look up at him. His eyes are hooded and suddenly his offer takes on a whole new meaning. He doesn't just look handsome; he looks downright sexy, and his invite is suggestive now of something more than just a drink. I fight my body's natural desire to step toward him and pull my fingers from his grasp. 'Another time.'

Another time? Why the fuck did I say that? Brilliant. I could have just said no. I could have said no chance. I could have told him we needed to keep this professional but no, no. I've left the fucking door open to continue this dance and make my job a whole lot fucking harder.

I dip into my bag, grab my keys and throw him a quick grin as I turn and walk out of his office.

'You're way too good for him, you know, Jen?'

'I'm way too good for you, Tristan.'

And I continue walking out of the office, head to my car and fall in exhausted. Today has been a revelation to say the least. My poor brain was already frazzled from hearing the conversations between Eddie and Angel this morning, and now this? I knew bad things happened in the world, but I guess with my life and how I choose to live it, I've remained blind to most of it – I hear snippets from the little news I watch and leave it at that. My life is and has always been one of first-world problems – all about making enough money to treat myself to luxuries and paying for my pony. I now feel like I've been thrown to the wolves in an underworld that doesn't belong on my radar. I'm struggling to comprehend not only everything that's actually going on in our beautiful town but also that it's been going on right under my nose.

I wonder how many times Eddie has been shoeing Lincoln with drugs in the back of his van? I wonder how many times he's dropped drugs off on his way to me or once he'd left me?

I wonder what they have on him to make him so frightened that he couldn't possibly leave? I know he's not just doing it to keep an eye on Angel. He's involved too. I heard what Angel said. What's more worrying is how the police, our local protection officers, know what's going on and are actually involved themselves. Should I really be getting involved in this? Is this going to prove dangerous to my own existence?

I look up instinctively at the windows of the office building above and there's Tristan, looking down on me.

He smiles through the glass and raises his hand, waving a phone in it. As he does, mine pings.

TRISTAN: Stop ogling me and fuck off home, gorgeous.

. . .

JEN: Piss off, Boss.

TRISTAN: YOU KNOW CALLING ME 'BOSS' is such a fucking turn-on.

JEN: Goodnight, Boss

I JUST CAN'T HELP myself, can I?

FIFTEEN

PULLING UP OUTSIDE THE FLAT, I take a deep
breath and stretch against my steering wheel. Today's been
a long day and I'm not quite sure how I'm going to deal with
this new world I seem to have found myself in, but I know
I'm going to give it my best bloody shot.

I unclip my seat belt and grab my bag from the
passenger seat, but as I go to step out the car, I'm pulled
back when the handle gets caught on the handbrake. I look
round and unhook it before turning back to step onto the
street, but my vision is suddenly blocked by the crotch of his
trousers. If I wasn't so tired I probably would have leapt out
of my skin. I guess I've spent too long around horses. Tire
them out and they become a little fresh, a little less spooky. I
guess that's what Tristan's done. He's frazzled my mind,
schooled me until I'm too tired to nap or spook at the sight
of Eddie's crotch in my face.

'What are you doing here?'

'Waiting for you obviously.'

'Ooh I feel honoured. Come to tell me to quit my job
again?'

I get out the car, making him step back to give me room, slam the door shut and hit the key fob. The internal mechanisms instantly lock shut, much like my heart whenever Eddie is present now. I turn to walk toward my flat and find myself having to walk around him.

He grunts at me and follows behind.

'What do you want, Ed?'

'We need to talk.'

'I'm tired. I've had a long day, learning about our local drug problem.'

He speeds up to get himself next to me and puts his hand around the top of my arm, making me walk faster than I was previously. 'Hey, what the fuck are you doing?'

'Just get inside now.'

He takes the keys out of my hand and uses the fob to open the security doors, pushing me inside, then following quickly behind.

'Are we being watching Ed or something?'

'I'd rather not run the risk.'

He marches me up the communal stairwell and opens my front door, pushing me in before it's even fully open.

'Now just what the fuck is going on?'

He kicks the door closed behind him and puts his hand on my face, his thumb under my chin. He takes a second or two, just looking at me, as if checking it's me, and then pulls me to him. His lips touch mine and it's nothing short of fireworks. But it's not what's meant to be happening.

I try to push him off me but he grabs my hands, then shoves me against the wall with his body, his lips fighting to find mine. He moves one of my hands into his other, holding on to both in just one of his. Though he has me pinned against the wall, I feel powerful, and when he puts his hand on my neck to stop me from evading his kiss, his lips finally find mine.

'Jen, stop fighting this,' he breathes through his rough, forceful kiss.

He may see me fight but he doesn't feel my body instinctively respond to his touch. My nipples harden, my breath shortens and pussy's now soaking wet for his touch.

I moan into his mouth, no longer able to hide my burning desire for him, and with that, he releases my hands and sends his hand down the front of my trousers instead. His other hand still around my neck, he bites down on my bottom lip as his fingers slide down the front of me, finding their way between my lips. They glide with ease through my wetness and begin circling slowly.

'Tell me you don't want this. Tell me you don't want me.'

I push my pelvis forward, to try to push his fingers further into me. It's like admitting I do want him, I do want this, without me having to actually say it.

'That's right, Jen, you fucking want this, don't you?'

His grip on my neck tightens and he pulls away from the wall, spinning me round before slamming me back against it. This time his body is crushing me against it too. His slides his hand back around and down my knickers again to slip two fingers inside of me, pushing in hard. And he does it again and again before he slides back and starts circling around my already sensitive clit.

I push my head back onto him and beg, 'Fuck me please.'

'I'll fuck your mouth first, baby, then I'll fuck you until your knees buckle.'

He pulls me off the wall, removes his hand from my knickers and turns me around to face him.

'Don't ever tell me you can't be with me, that you can be without this.'

He kisses me, rounds his hands on my arse and picks me up. My legs know exactly where they're supposed to be and wrap themselves around his waist. He walks blind to my bedroom, and as he does I throw my jacket to the floor before pulling my vest over my head, kicking my heels off as he gets to my bed and throws me down. He's at my trousers now, and in one clean tug, they're off and on the other side of the room.

He leans over me, one hand beside my head, and traces the other down between my breast, over my stomach to the top of my knickers. He looks back up at my breasts and pulls each bra cup down to reveal both rock-hard nipples, just waiting for his attention. He leans in, sucking and biting them, and I arch my back in response to the immeasurable pleasure I get from his harsh ministrations.

He lets my breasts drop from his mouth through his teeth before looking once more at my knickers. He trails his finger down again and skims the waist band then runs his finger over the top of my knickers before taking it down to the crotch, where he pulls at the seam and slips a finger underneath.

'So very fucking wet for me, aren't you?'

'Yes. Yes. Fuck me now.'

'You said please before? You not going to say please again, baby?'

'Please, Eddie. Fuck me *please.*'

I'm amazed at how quickly I turn so desperate for him. How much I need him as soon as his lips touch mine. All reason is lost. I become all consumed by him, unable to put logic first because my body calls out for him, as if it's a missing piece that's finally come home.

He grabs my shoulders and slides me off the bed, where I fall to my knees. He pulls his T-shirt over his head to reveal a muscular body that looks nothing short of pumped right now, on the verge of fucking exploding, and I grab his belt. He pushes the hair from my face and holds it behind my head.

I leave the belt dangling either side of his fly, undo his jeans and push them and his boxers down just enough for his cock to burst out, nearly hitting me in the face. I lean back, looking at its thickness, the veins running along the shaft, and see the wetness at the very end. I lap the precum up and take the very base of the shaft in my hand.

'Oh fuck me, Jen, don't stop.' His grip on my hair tightens and he pushes into me with force.

I gag, splutter but take him all in, sucking hard. The power I feel with his hard cock in my mouth is like nothing else. I move up and down his shaft, licking and nibbling as I go, my hand closely following suit. I move fast, gaining momentum before I stop and focus my attention on his head, licking up the wetness that just keeps on escaping.

He leaves one hand on my head and moves the other down to pinch and pull at my breasts, and fuck me it feels good. I moan, which sends vibrations down his cock, which is almost his undoing as he hisses at me, 'Slow down, baby, slow down. Don't make me come yet – I need to fuck you so hard you can't possibly walk away from me again.'

And with that, he picks me up under one arm and slings me down on the bed. I wipe his precum from my mouth and look up at him. His face has changed – he looks like a predator who's caught his prey, and fuck me do I want to be ripped apart by him right now.

Before I have a chance to move, he flips me over and pushes my head down on the bed, my arse rising instantly in response. I crave him. It's natural. I have to accept the fact that there's just no fighting this attraction between us.

As my arse rises to meet his cock, he pulls my kickers aside and smashes into my wet and wanting pussy on a growl. I scream with nothing but pleasure and beg for more.

He pumps into me hard before lifting me up, his hand around my neck. He continues to pump into me as he brings my face around to meet his so he can ravage me with his tongue as much as he is with his cock.

His other hand now slips beneath my soaking-wet knickers, working on my clit. I start to feel the heat rise through my body, and the otherworldly feeling that begins to take over.

The vibrations start and he orders me, 'Take it, take it, fucking cum for me,' and it's all I need to tip me over the edge, my body overtaken with this pure, carnal desire. My knees give up but I hang there, by my neck, as he continues to fuck me raw, growling like an animal before I feel him beginning to pulse inside of me.

'God you're squeezing me. Fuck me, I'm gonna cum, Jen. I'm gonna—' And just like that, he releases everything into me. He fills me up, and unable to hold me up anymore, we both collapse onto the bed, him lying across my back, still solid inside of me, panting over my whole body.

We're a hot sweaty mess, and right now, it's exactly where I want to be. Exactly where I *need* to be. The fact that he's caught up in a seedy and dangerous world isn't even on my radar at the moment. I just want to be here, right now, like this. I'll lock my door, we'll order food and pretend the outside world doesn't exist.

SIXTEEN

I PULL my hot sticky body from underneath him. He doesn't like me leaving him but he flips over onto his side, his now flaccid penis falling to the side, and watches me walk to the bathroom. I feel him dripping out of me and pull off my now-sodden knickers before I flick on the shower and step in, starting to rinse myself off as soon as the water warms up a little. I feel the steam escape as the door opens and he slips in behind me. His arm comes around my waist and he kisses my shoulder, his other arm curling around my chest.

'I've missed you. You broke my heart this morning, Jen.'

'You think you didn't shatter mine? You need to tell me what's going on.'

'I will – I'll tell you everything, but you have to promise not to run away from me when I do.'

I turn to look him in the eyes as he says this.

We finish washing each other off. He suds my hair before lathering up his own and for a few minutes we're smiling, with just a glimmer of the banter we used to have before this all became so serious. So dangerous.

We dry each other off, and he plays around, goofily trying to dry in between my legs. We giggle like teenagers. But we aren't teenagers. We're adults who are both now involved in something very serious and very sinister.

I throw on a baggy jumper and some tracksuit bottoms.

'Wow – sexy, Jen! Such an effort you're making while you've got your new bloke at yours. Isn't it supposed to be a few years down the line before you start slacking?'

'Let's see if you make it a few years down the line first, shall we?' I instantly regret the words, and the silence in the room only emphasises that I definitely said the wrong thing.

'Cup of tea?' The very British response to any awkward moment.

'Yeah, sure.' Thank fuck it works and words are uttered. Christ alive this is going to be tough.

'So... you going to start talking or what?'

'Yeah, definitely. Umm. Well, where do you want me to start?'

'Why are you drug running for the Drafter brothers?'

'Oh fuck me, Jen – dive right in.' He throws his head into his hands and rubs his face, as if trying to muster some energy or even just figure out where to start before landing on my three-seater sofa and leaning back.

'When I was a teenager, my mum got really ill. My dad wasn't around and I was struggling to pay the bills. To pay for her care. As soon as she left the hospital, I was told she had to go into a home. We were renting and because I was working, I wanted to pay toward her care. If the state paid for it, she'd end up in this shitty care home that would barely keep her alive. If I paid toward it, she'd get moved into a better care home and get a better level of care. I mean it was a no-brainer. The only trouble was the size of the bills – every fucking week too.

'Back then I mixed with some unscrupulous crowds, shall we say, and I knew Damion and Alfie before they became the notorious Drafter brothers you know. Before they'd made it on the scene. I guess I was their first plaything.'

'What do you mean plaything?' I sit myself down on the chair opposite him. I want space between us while he explains.

'They lent me money, said they'd help because our mums knew each other and that. I stupidly believed them, but I wanted to pay it back. They refused at first and then things took a bit of a nasty turn. I ended up in so much debt to them that they essentially owned me. There was no running away. They would find me eventually. So I had to pay up.'

'And how did you pay up exactly?' I know the answer but I need him to tell me.

'I'd built a fairly decent client base at yards around the south of the country by then.' He looks down at his hands, rubbing them, fiddling with his fingers, and I realise he's nervous. 'And so I started delivering packages for them.' He makes air quotes as he says the word *packages*.

'Drugs. You started drug running.'

'Yes. They didn't tell me it was drugs, just that they needed a delivery man of sorts and I was that man. Once I'd done it a few times, they had me. You can't just enter that world and leave without some kind of consequence. I thought about ways I could stop it all the time, and then I saw them bring their sister in when she turned sixteen.'

'Oh bloody lovely – at least they waited until she was fucking legal.'

'They brought her in, Jen, not me. As soon as I saw what was going on, I was warned off getting involved and made very aware of what would happen if I did. So I stuck around to kind of ensure she was OK, I suppose – not that I can make what was being done to her OK, but you know what I mean.

'That's why I got her livery at your yard. I shoe all fifty-five horses there so I'm there every single week to check on her, keep an eye on her, make sure she's OK.

'She's not a bad woman, you know. She's just been used and abused by the people who are supposed to protect her.'

'No wonder she's such a bitch then.'

I lean back in my chair and stare at the ceiling. 'What did you mean that you just needed a month or something?'

'I think I might have a way out but I just need you to trust me. Jen, I know this is your work, your job, but you're getting involved in something that goes way beyond Langley, and I'm worried you're going to put yourself at risk. Angel has already told her brothers about you, out of spite after yesterday, and I'm worried they're going to start watching you. They know I'm not happy and that I want out.'

He leans forward on his seat and looks down at his hands.

'They also know how I feel about you, Jen. I can't have you coming to any harm.'

I have nothing left to say, nothing to say that will make him feel better, because I'm already involved. I'm already digging where I shouldn't be and finding out things I shouldn't. So all I can do is what I know will make him feel better. And me for that matter.

I get up and walk toward him. I place one knee by his hip and lift my other over him, so I'm straddling him, pushing him back against the sofa, then place both my hands on either side of his face and kiss him tenderly. He reaches up and cups each of my butt cheeks, lifting me ever so slightly – just enough for him to slide sideways and lie me down on his long body.

And that's how we spend the rest of the evening, connected, all consumed, avoiding what's really happening outside of my flat. We're here, in our safe bubble, and that's where we'll stay until we need to face another day.

SEVENTEEN

THE ALARM GOES off and I turn over in bed. I don't know when we made it into the bed, but we spent time on the sofa, back on the kitchen worktop and even back in the shower at one point before we fell into bed. The man knows how to please a woman, that's for sure.

I roll over and find him nowhere to be seen. In his place though is a note with a smiley face and a heart. I guess all the talking last night left him with nothing left in his vocabulary, though considering the situation we both find ourselves in, there isn't much left to say just now.

I spend the rest of my day writing and then relax in the bath, trying to soak my worn-out muscles from our marathon of passion, as I've dubbed it.

My phone pings from where it sits on the toilet-seat lid.

LIV: Remember – Hogan's tonight at 7 p.m. See you there, Little Miss Slutty.

. . .

I CRINGE at the Little Miss Slutty. Oh she's going to give me some grief tonight. I knew I should have left it until tonight to tell her about last night. But when it comes to Liv, I just can't help but spill the beans.

JEN: I shouldn't have bloody told you. See you tonight.

LIV: What you wearing... oh wait, let me guess. Jeans and a nice top?

JEN: Sarcastic bitch. Laters.

I GET READY, throwing a few curls in my hair and slapping a little make-up on before making my way out to my waiting cab. I'm definitely going to be having a drink tonight, especially if Liv's going to make me relive it all as I tell her everything that's going on. She's even raised a few eyebrows when it comes to Tristan, though I can't say I'm surprised after I described him as 'completely fuckable'.

I talk to the cab driver. Ask him all the usual, mind-numbingly boring questions that you usually ask.

'Have you been on shift long?'

'Has it been busy tonight?'

'What time you on till?'

We have a little natter about the weather and then he pulls up directly outside Hogan's. Before I jump out, I throw a £10 note into his hand and thank him for the safe journey, telling him to keep the £3 as a tip. He nods his appreciation and I head into the bar, hit with the noise as the main doors open up for me. I say hey to the bouncers, who know my face well enough by now, and then make my way to our usual spot, where I find Liv frantically typing on her phone.

'Hey, what's going on. You look pissed off?'

'Fucking Damion has messaged out of the blue, wanting to meet up.'

'You're not going to, are you?'

'Am I fuck!'

I love her spunk. She's so fiery it's amazing. Her personality matches her vibrant red hair too. Pair it with her tight-arse bandeau dress and it's no wonder she's always drawing attention from every angle. I've already seen at least five men eyeing her up, just on my way over here, and no doubt she'll get chatting with a guy tonight who'll she decide to either shag or shift (get rid of) as she calls it.

We spend most of the evening chatting, discussing what's actually going on. None of which comes as a surprise to Liv, considering her previous connection with Damion and the fact that she's far more worldly than I am.

'Jen, I have absolute faith that you'll make all the right decisions. If you want to shag Eddie, you shag Eddie, love. Likewise, this Tristan sounds like a fucking dish. I'm your best mate, babe – you know that – so I'm here to support you, whatever you do, not tell you what to do, but right now, I have to say, I'm really uncomfortable with you writing this story. I'm guessing that's why Damion has decided he'd like to see me again. They aren't stupid – they have a lot of connections, Jen. They'll know you're getting involved, and if, like Eddie says, they now know you two are involved... well. I just see an unavoidable ticking time bomb, my babe.' She takes a big swig of her large white wine, almost drinking the entire serving whole.

I look around, suddenly feeling uneasy. The enormity of what I could be getting myself into has left me feeling cold. I have goosebumps and can't shift the feeling that I'm being watched.

If this is how I feel after just a warning from my best friend, then fuck me, what am I going to feel like if I actually bump into these guys?

'Can we talk about something else?' I look around the bar as I bring my glass to my lips and try my best to shift this uneasy feeling.

'Yeah, of course we can. Come on, we've come out to have a good night. I'll run to the bar and grab us a couple of shots and another couple of wines. You stop crossing your legs and get to the toilet before you piss yourself and then we'll have a dance. I might even throw my handbag on the floor and dance around it, just to be a wanky prick.'

She winks at me and clucks my cheek, ever the mothering one in our friendship. I put my glass on the table and turn toward her, soaking up the attention.

I hadn't noticed I was shifting in my seat, and now I definitely need the loo. How does she bloody do that?

The table shifts as someone bumps into it, nearly knocking over my glass. I quickly pick it up and swill it around before I down the last mouthful. Then I slide off the chair and make my way to the toilets, squeezing between groups of friends, couples and people obviously on their first date. Some dates look great, others look bloody awkward. I make a mental note to share my observations with Liv when I meet her at the bar. We love people watching more than anything. We like to dissect what we can see and try our best to work out the dynamics between them, basically making up any old crap.

I stumble into the hall where the toilets are, feeling flushed.

The rush of cool air on my face feels amazing, but I can't shift this hot feeling. I look toward where the breeze is coming from and notice the door that goes out to the beer garden is wide open, but no one's actually out there. I thought they were renovating...

I turn toward the toilets and bump into someone. Apologising instantly, before I even see who it is, I find myself face to face with Angel.

'I told you to stay away from him, Jen. You're going to cause me a whole world of problems if you won't take a bit of notice.'

'What? What the fuck are you talking about?' I stumble, suddenly feeling less than sturdy. My body feels so hot. The heat feels almost like its spreading up from chest, and I suddenly feel incredibly drunk despite only having had one glass of wine.

I fumble behind me, trying desperately to grab anything that might keep me upright. I can't stand up straight. I kick my heels off and look to Angel, who's now been joined by two men. I don't see their faces but the sudden realisation of who they are sinks in.

'What have you done, Angel?'

My body feels limp and as I fall, I see one of the shadows of the men step toward me.

My eyes feel heavy and I fight to stop them from closing. I know I'm stopped from hitting the ground. I drop my bag, my arms going limp, and as they do, my eyes close and my world goes dark...

ACKNOWLEDGEMENTS

This book has been a work in progress for as long as I can remember. I've had the story in my brain for at least four years and finally gathered a rough idea of a front cover back in 2018. I remember vividly, sitting under an umbrella in a huge Storm in Orlando, Florida, on holiday with my husband, my then 3 year old daughter and our new 3 month old daughter. We were coming to the end of our holiday and as always, I'd made big plans regarding our lives, what was going to change and how I was going to make that happen. I haphazardly threw together a basic front cover on Canva, which the marvellous Francessca Wingfield would later create for me to look a million times better than I could have ever envisioned.

Despite this, the story remained firmly in my mind for another 18 months before I threw it together.

While I would have loved to have got this story out when I first concurred it up, I'm a firm believer that everything happens for a reason and everything happens *when* it's meant to happen.

Our experiences in life, good and bad, are what make us and the last two years have without a doubt made me a much stronger, far more capable person. Without that fire inside of me, I don't think Soaked Hay & Farrier Smoke would have packed quite as big a punch.

I'd like to thank the incredible aforementioned Francessca Wingfield for her amazing vision for the front cover and the super talented Laura Kincaid for her awesome editing skills. Without both of these guys, I would never have been able to create anything quite so professional in appearance or verse. They are simply fabulous.

I'd like to thank my parents who gave birth to the legend that is me... I'm kidding. I'd like to thank them for being so supportive and genuinely getting behind me writing "smut" as my father refers to it, despite the fact they'll likely never read it. My mum most definitely needs her own mention for the sheer fact that she's told me from a very early age, "You need to write! You write such great stories." Thank you mum.

Another thank you must go out to Elizabeth Davies, the designer and owner of Vivendi Apparel, which if you've read this far you will recognise as the brand of leggings that Jen wears with the incredible silicone wings. You've been a huge support, giving me not only a job that enabled me to leave my public services career, but also now becoming my partner in VH Collective and ultimately being an incredible source of business knowledge and expertise... considering we've never physically met, it's bloody crazy.

Last but not least (we always save the best for last right?), I'd like to take the time to thank my husband Rob. Without him, I'd never have begun writing. I'm incredibly lucky to have had his full support in leaving behind a 14 year career in the public services, regardless of whether I ever sell a single copy of my book. Having that support has been nothing short of life changing. He's not only a fantastic husband but an amazing dad AND he has helped me some how collect a 5 strong herd of stunning equines, all while keeping me topped up on chocolate, tea and diet coke for the entire duration of my writing this book. I couldn't ask for a better partner in my life. Here's to another fantastic 10 years together with my very own lead man.

Cover Design: Francessca Wingfield - https://www.facebook.com/FrancesscasPRandDesigns
Editing: Laura Kincaid - https://www.tenthousand.co.uk/
Tea Maker: Rob Hyde - www.fitfob.com

Soaked Hay & Stable Mirrors Book 2

Of course, as you will have realised, this isn't the end of the story for Jen, Eddie and the Soaked Hay bunch. The second instalment of this incredible duo series will be released in November. If you'd like to read more, please do sign up to my newsletter or check out my social media links below where I'll be releasing updates and links to preorder Soaked Hay & Stable Mirrors.

I can't wait for you to see how the story ends for Eddie & Jen. I can only hope that I've concluded their story in a way the characters and you, the reader, deserve.

Get to know me more here...
Instagram - https://www.
instagram.com/thefairweatherrider/
Facebook - https://www.facebook.com/thefairweatherrider
Website - http://thefairweatherrider.com

COPYRIGHT